MW00987586

SNIPPETS (Book Two)
How the Civil War Changed the Lives of: Jesse James; Johnny Clem, The "Little" Drummer Boy of Chickamauga; Elizabeth Thorn, The "Angel" of Gettysburg; The Younger Boys; and Belle Boyd, The "Cleopatra of Secession"

July 22, 2023

For Dad. With love.

These stories are works of fiction. However, they are based heavily on fact and are, therefore, not politically correct.

To Susan,

Enjoy!

Diane

OTHER BOOKS BY D.L. ROGERS

*SNIPPETS: A Compilation of Historical and
Contemporary Short Stories – Book One;
50 SOMETHING: Death, Divorce & Menopause;
Perils on the Missouri: A Tale of Life and Death
Along the Big Muddy;
Treachery at Midnight: A Daughter's
Remembrances of the Civil War, Wayside Rest and
her (Special) Friendship with Cole Younger;
Bury Me with My People: The Arrests of Elizabeth
Temms and the Roswell Mill Workers;
Fire on the Horizon: The Death of the Morro
Castle;
Lou's Story: She Adder or Patriot?;
Crossfire in the Street: Lone Jack 1862;
Elizabeth's War: Missouri 1863;*

THE WHITE OAKS SERIES

*Beginnings: Into the Unknown;
Tomorrow's Promise: Survival on the Plains; Caleb;
Brothers by Blood; Amy; Ghost Dancers; Maggie;
THE OLD COOTS: Sam;
THE OLD COOTS: Tom;
THE OLD COOTS: Blue, Gray & Gold
Echoes in the Dark* – Vietnam Era Fiction
The Journey – A Romance

Cover Design by: Glen Dixon
DLRogersBooks, LLC / www.dlrogersbooks.com

Frank's Childish Prank

1862, The Wornall Estate, Kansas City, Missouri

Seven-year-old Frank Wornall dropped to his knees on the outer, second-floor, balcony of his family's home. He gripped the deck rails and peered down at the mounted men passing on the street below. "Who are they?" he asked Mittie Pigg, the teenaged orphan girl from Kentucky his father had taken in when her parents were killed who acted as a servant to earn her keep.

"Don't you know?" she whispered her eyes wide.

Frank shook his head. He turned to face her. "Do you?"

Mittie studied the troops on the road then pointed through the rails. "See them blue uniforms? That makes 'em Yankees. The ones fightin' the Confederates to get rid of slavery," she told him.

Frank shivered. "We got slaves. Does that mean them boys want to fight my papa?"

"They want to tell your papa how to live." A strange gleam came into her eyes. "I bet you're afeared of them soldiers."

"Am not." Frank stiffened his back in challenge.

"Then I dare you to yell at 'em. Show 'em you're not afraid."

Frank sat back on his heels and puffed out his chest. He didn't want Mittie to think he was just a dumb little boy. Or chicken. "What do you want me to yell?"

She pursed her lips, pondered a moment, then said, "Hurrah for Jeff Davis!"

Frank didn't know who Jeff Davis was, but he must be someone special to those soldiers, he decided. He jumped to his feet, pumped his fist, and yelled, "Hurrah for Jeff Davis!"

The riders jerked their mounts to a halt and swiveled their heads to glare up at Frank and Mittie. Frank knew right away that whoever Jeff Davis was, these men didn't like him. Their faces looked like thunderclouds about to explode.

Fear washed over Frank. He was only five two years ago when the war had started. He knew men were fighting each other. Even though his mama and papa tried to keep him from knowing what was going on, he heard things.

He'd stand on the other side of the parlor door and listen when they talked about the war. Mama often scolded Papa for doing business with the Yankees, but Papa said he was a businessman and that he did whatever had to be done to keep his family and home safe. If that meant being nice to the Yankees, then that was what he would do.

Those soldiers below didn't look like friends to his papa. They looked ready to fight.

Frank stood frozen on the porch, wishing Mittie hadn't dared him. Maybe he *was* just a stupid boy. He waited for the soldiers to yell back or ride into the yard and take him away.

The Yankees didn't stop, but gave him angry looks as they passed. After the last rider disappeared, Frank slumped to the floor. "Why did you make me do that?" he asked Mittie when she scooted beside him.

Mittie merely shrugged. "Don't know. Thought it'd be funny, I guess." She cocked her head. "Didn't think they'd take it so poorly."

"Who is Jeff Davis anyway?"

Mittie frowned. "Only the president of the Confederacy."

Frank felt his face heat. "Were you *tryin'* to get me in trouble?"

Mittie shrugged. "No, but—"

"Well, it weren't funny and we're lucky they didn't come git me." Frank stood on wobbly legs. He turned his back to Mittie and stalked into the house. His hands rolled in and out of fists as he went. He was madder than a cat tossed into a pond. He wanted to yell at Mittie. Tell her how bad her foolishness made him feel. Instead, he went to his room and cried.

***

That night after dinner, Mittie came up behind Frank in the parlor and tapped him on the shoulder. When he turned around, she said, "I'm sorry, Frankie. No harm come from our little joke." She nudged him with her shoulder. "They did look like one giant thunderhead, though, didn't they?" she added with a giggle.

Frank couldn't keep himself from chuckling with her when he recalled how mad the soldiers looked. "They didn't do anything this time. But don't you go daring me again."

Mittie spat on the palm of her hand and put it out for Frank to do the same. He did and they shook on their truce.

Frank's mother, Eliza, entered the parlor. Mittie and Frank quickly released hands and stepped away from each other. Mrs. Wornall lifted her eyebrows in curiosity, then glanced over at her husband, engrossed in a book he was reading across the room. She sighed.

"Why don't you children play The Game of Life to pass the evening?" she told Mittie and Frank.

"Wanna?" Mittie asked Frank.

Frank shrugged. "Why not." He liked Mittie and didn't want her to think of him as a little boy. He wanted to impress her, as he'd so foolishly tried to do earlier. He would even play a game he wasn't sure how to play.

Mittie pulled out the game and set it up. Although Frank read well for his age, some of the squares on the board confused him. He knew the good ones to land on were "School-to-College," "Bravery," and "Fame," but he wasn't so sure about some of the others he sounded out like "Prison," "Pov...er...ty," and "Dis...grace."

He played along as well as he could but, before long, Mittie was whipping him.

His mother must have seen his frustration because she put her knitting aside. "It's getting late. Time for bed, Frank."

"Aw, Mama. Do I have to?"

Frank's father laid down his book. "Listen to your mother, Frank. It's time to find your bed. Go on now."

Frank jumped to his feet. "I didn't want to play that silly game anymore anyway."

"Don't be like that, young man," his father chastised.

Frank hung his head. "Sorry, Sir. Good night, Papa. Mama." He gave them each a kiss on the cheek and padded up the stairs to his room. Mittie started toward her attic room above, but his mama's firm, "Mittie, stay. We need to talk," halted her.

Frank wondered what his mama wanted to talk to Mittie about but put it out of his mind. After the day he'd had, he was looking forward to his bed. He washed up, slid into his night shirt, and crawled between the sheets. He was asleep in minutes.

He had no idea how long he'd been abed when voices downstairs woke him.

Fear zipped up his spine. They were not the voices of his mother or father. Not even Mittie's. And they sounded angry.

He threw off the covers, rolled out of bed, and ran down the stairs. He jerked to a stop on the lower landing when four soldiers came into view in the parlor. Soldiers wearing the same blue uniforms as the men he'd yelled at this afternoon. Yankees.

Frank felt like his feet were stuck in the mud. His heart hammered and he shivered. Why were these soldiers here? Treating his papa like he'd done something wrong? Were they here because of what he'd yelled? He grabbed the stair rail to keep from falling.

"I swear to you, Sir, it was just a childish prank," Frank's father told the soldiers. "My son is only seven and had no idea what he was yelling. I'm sure he doesn't even know who Jeff Davis is."

"It sounded like he knew to me and my men. Like it's a name he hears often in this household."

"I assure you, it is not," Frank's father responded. "We do our best to shield him from war talk."

Mittie came down the stairs and stopped behind Frank.

Frank turned to her. "I have to tell them my papa didn't do anything." Tears filled his eyes and his lower lip trembled.

Mittie's face flamed red. She frowned. "I already told your ma and pa why you yelled at them soldiers. That I dared you."

Frank stiffened. "You did?"

"Your ma know'd something was wrong between us tonight. That's why she wanted to talk to me when you went up to bed."

"That soldier doesn't believe Papa. He keeps telling that soldier you dared me and that we didn't mean nothing by it, but he won't listen." More than ever, Frank felt like a stupid boy. "I gotta tell them it was me and only me. That Papa had nothing to do with any of it," Frank whined. "He didn't even know what I done."

He took a step, but Mittie grabbed his arm to keep him from going farther down the stairs. "There's nothin' you can do, Frank," she hissed in his ear. "Just let your pa take care of it."

"But they don't believe him," Frank cried. He studied the soldier in the parlor whose face was only inches from his father's.

"I ain't got no love loss for your kind, John Wornall. I know all about you. You hold slaves, yet you profess to be a Union man when it suits you." The soldier stepped closer. "It doesn't suit tonight." He paused a moment then added, "Maybe a little neck-stretching might loosen your tongue with the truth."

Mittie wrapped her arms around Frank's slender shoulders to keep him from charging down the stairs and into the room.

"My husband is telling you the truth," Frank's mama cried out when she stepped between the soldier and her husband. "My son was merely reacting to a dare by a girl he likes. He meant no harm."

"Tell that to my men who rode the rest of the way waiting for an ambush because of your son's 'childish prank,' as your husband calls it."

"But that's what it was," his mama said, her voice controlled like when she was trying not to yell. "A childish prank. My son is a mere boy. He didn't even know who Jeff Davis was."

"I bet he knows now," the soldier doing all the talking said. He grabbed Frank's father by the arm and led him toward the front door. "We'll see what the lieutenant says when we get back to camp."

"Camp?" Frank's mama cried out. "He's innocent. You have no right to take him."

Frank's papa turned to his mother. "Eliza. Stop. They're set on taking me. Don't worry, I'll convince their lieutenant I did nothing wrong."

Frank's mother ran to his father and grabbed him around the waist. They had to wrench him from her arms to drag him out the front door.

"I'll be back, Eliza. I promise. I'll convince them how wrong this is. Trust me."

The door slammed shut. Frank's papa was gone.

*

"Go on back up to bed now, Frank. There's nothing that can be done except wait," Frank's mother told him.

He opened his mouth to argue, but snapped it shut with the glare she gave him.

"Yes, Mama." He turned on his heel and started up the stairs.

"You go up too," she told Mittie.

Frank could tell Mama was mad at Mittie by the tone of her voice. This was all Mittie's fault! If she hadn't dared him, his papa wouldn't have been taken away by the soldiers.

He trudged up the stairs like a ball and chain were attached to each of his ankles. Why had he listened to Mittie? Why wasn't he smart enough to know he shouldn't yell at soldiers? For any reason. Even to impress a girl. Now his papa was paying the price for his stupidity.

He sensed someone behind him and turned to find Mittie standing on the stair below him. She opened her mouth to speak, but he turned his back on her. "Leave me alone. I don't want you to talk to me. Ever again."

She grabbed his arm and stopped him from reaching the top of the stairs. "Please. Forgive me, Frank. I'm so sorry."

He whirled on her, ignoring the tears pooling in her eyes. "Here I was thinking I was the stupid one. But you're the stupid one. You! Why did you tell me to do something so dumb? You said you thought it would be funny. Well, it's not funny! And my papa…" He couldn't say the words because he didn't fully understand what might happen to his father.

"That one soldier asked Papa if he wanted his neck stretched. Does that mean they're going to hang him? For what I did?" Frank swallowed the lump that had formed in his throat. He might be only seven, but he knew what happened when someone was hanged.

He dropped to his knees on the stairs and began to sob. "I didn't mean to get Papa in trouble. I didn't mean it."

Mittie cradled him in her arms and tried to console him.

She was the last person he wanted to make him feel better. He shoved her away and got to his feet. "Don't touch me and don't talk to me I told you. Just leave me alone." He ran up the last few stairs to his room and slammed the door in Mittie's face when she followed.

Frank cried and cried. He couldn't stop, he was so afraid of what might happen to his father. He had no idea how long he'd been crying when he heard something that jerked him upright.

The front door.

He jumped up, tore out of his room and down the stairs. In the entryway, his papa had his arms wrapped around his mama. She was sobbing into his chest.

"Papa!" Frank leapt down the last two stairs. He ran to his father. Slammed into him with a loud "oof."

Mr. Wornall released his wife and lifted Frank into the air. "I'm home, Son. I'm home."

"Oh, Papa, I was so scared." He touched his father's face to make sure he was real.

When Frank's father set his feet on the floor, he turned to see Mittie coming down the stairs. Anger ripped through him, but he held it inside.

"I'm so glad you're home, Mr. Wornall. I was so worried."

Frank's Papa stepped toward the teenaged girl he'd given a home. "I hope this is a lesson to you, Mittie. This war is not a game. These soldiers take this business very seriously." He lifted an eyebrow at her.

"Yes, Sir. I've certainly learned a lesson. I don't know what overcome me, but I'll never do anything like that again." She fell into Mr. Wornall's arms sobbing.

Mr. Wornall shushed her, then held her back from him and told her it was all right. "It took a while, but those soldiers finally believed me that it was just a childish prank." He eyed Mittie harshly. "One I promised would never be repeated."

"No, Sir. I mean yes, Sir. I'll never do it again. Never. I swear it on my dead parents' grave." She crossed her heart with her finger.

Mr. Wornall turned to Frank. "And have you learned a lesson today too?" he asked his son.

"Yes, Papa."

"And what lesson was that?"

"Don't take a Mittie Pigg dare!"

Afterword

The previous short story is taken from a description of what happened to young Frank Wornall in a display at the Wornall House in Kansas City, Missouri, as follows:

"Frank's Mistake"

"Childhood on the American frontier was much different than it is today. For children like Frank Wornall (b. 1855), the violence of the Border War was an ever-present fact of life.

"Frank was only seven years old in 1862, when he inadvertently brought the ire of federal troops down upon his father. One day, young Frank was standing on th[is] second-story balcony with Mittie Pigg, a teenaged orphan girl from Kentucky that John had brought to stay with the family. As a company of Union soldiers passed the house, traveling north on what is now Wornall Road, the girl said: 'Frank, I dare you to shout 'Hurrah for Jeff Davis [the president of the Confederacy].'" Frank explained what happened next in his memoirs:

"I was at an age when I would take a dare, so in a piping voice I shouted. The passing soldiers looked our way but did not stop; however, that night after I had gone to bed and was asleep, a part of the troop returned, and refusing to listen to father's explanation, marched him away with a threat of death.

"Eliza (Mrs. Wornall) had gotten Mittie to confess to what had happened, and John desperately tried to explain Frank's actions as a childish prank; he must have been convincing, because the soldiers allowed him to return home that night."

The "Game of Life," played by Mittie and Frank the night John Wornall was taken away, was created by Milton Bradley in **1860**. Like many popular nineteenth-century games, it was meant to teach a moral lesson about proper behavior. The goal was to land on "good" spaces to collect points, with the winner being the first to gather 100 points. "Happy Old Age" is the highest scoring square, worth 50 points.

Photo taken by D.L. Rogers at the Wornall House, February 23, 2022.

The "Angel" Of Gettysburg

Elizabeth Thorn Statue at the Evergreen
Cemetery in Gettysburg

Elizabeth & Peter Thorn Wedding Photo
Photo taken from the internet
ELIZABETH THORN: "Those Were Hard Days"
By Diana Loski (author photo) (see references)
(Adams County Historical Society)
And America Comes Alive (see references)

Gatehouse (entry into the Gettysburg cemetery) where the Thorns lived. Peter & Elizabeth on the north side and her parents, John and Catherine Masser, on the south.
Photo taken from the internet (see references)
ELIZABETH THORN: "Those Were Hard Days"
By Diana Loski (author photo)

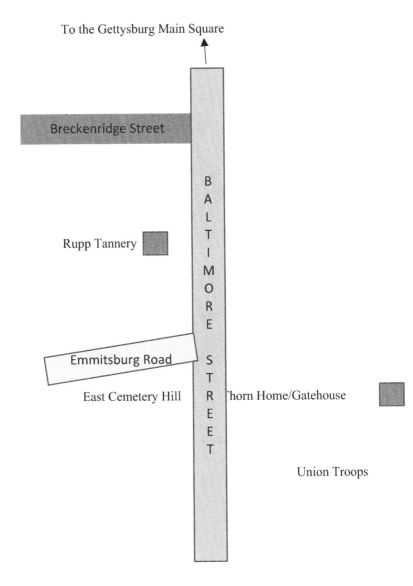

Rendered from Cindy L. Small's "Jennie Wade of Gettysburg. The Complete Story of the Only Civilian Killed During the Battle of Gettysburg."

The "Angel" of Gettysburg

February 1856

"Mutter!" Elizabeth Thorn shouted across the outdoor walkway in her native German. "I have the last of your things." She grunted from the weight of her burden. It was only a short distance between her parents' and her residence, but it seemed a mile with the weight she carried. She studied the stone archway above that joined hers and Peter's residence on the north side with that of her parents on the south.

The load shifted in her arms. "Hurry and open the door or I shall drop this box. It is very heavy!"

While she waited for her mother to come to the door, she thought back over how she'd come to be here. Although twenty-one years old and already a woman old enough to make her own decisions, Elizabeth had accompanied her parents when they left Germany months before to immigrate to America. She had not only left her hometown, but also the man she'd *thought* she would marry.

A smile curled her lips. Had she remained in the old country, she would never have met Peter Thorn. The wonderful man who had boarded the ship when they did, befriended them, and helped them acquire all new belongings upon arrival after everything had been stolen during their journey. After a six-month courtship, Peter became Elizabeth's husband on September 1, 1855. To their delight, he would soon become a father.

In early February of 1856, Peter had been offered the position of caretaker for the cemetery just outside of Gettysburg, Pennsylvania. So here they were. Moving her parents into one side of the caretaker residences and she and Peter into the other.

The door swung open. "Come in. Come in." Her mother waved Elizabeth inside and helped her set her burden on a chair beside the door.

Despite the February cold, Elizabeth was sweating under her coat. She shrugged it off, delighted the drudgery of getting their new homes in order was almost over.

Her mother made tea for them and chattered on about Peter and his new job and how lucky they were to have this wonderful place to live—rent free. It had been the right decision for Elizabeth to come here her mother reminded her for the hundredth time. She and Peter would build a good life. Raise a family. And be happy.

*

Six Years Later - August 1862

"Why now?" Elizabeth asked Peter. Her heart slammed in her chest at her husband's unexpected, and frightening, announcement. "You didn't join up when the war started last year. I thought you stayed home because of me and the children. Why would you enlist now?" She couldn't believe he intended to go.

Peter put his hands on her upper arms and led her to a chair. When she was seated, he pulled another chair in front of her and sat down, then took her hands in his.

"When the war started, no one believed it would last more than a few months. I didn't want to enlist only to be turned back as soon as I got wherever they sent me. I had you and our three young children to consider." He scrubbed at his face. "It is different now. The war has lasted so much longer than anyone expected. It is time to do my duty to my new country."

"Your duty?" she cried out. "What about your duty to our boys? To me? And my parents? They are getting old and need more help. How will we survive if you are gone?" She felt as though she stood teetering on a precipice, trying not to fall in.

"You shall take over my position as caretaker of the cemetery. You know what must be done as well as I do. I have already spoken with Mr. McConaughy and he agrees. So does your father. He said he will help."

"You've spoken to my father *and* Mr. McConaughy on this matter, but not me?"

"Let me remind you," Peter interrupted, "we have only four or five burials a month you would be responsible to take care of. I know you can do what must be done. Easily. In this way, you shall be paid for your duties and keep our family safe and fed while I am away."

Elizabeth pulled her arms back, breaking his hold on her. "It seems you have thought of everything."

Peter reached for her hands again. "Please understand, Elizabeth. This is something I must do. This country has given us a good life so I must do my duty to it. Do not fight me. My mind is made up." He sucked in a deep breath. "I have already enlisted with the 138th Pennsylvania Infantry. They are scheduled to recruit for another two days then move out. I shall leave in three days with them."

Elizabeth slumped in the chair. "Three days?" She felt as though she'd tumbled over the edge into the deep crevice.

"The Confederacy can't hold on forever. They can't replace the men they lose like the Union can. The war will end soon. I believe that." Peter squeezed her hands.

Elizabeth lifted her chin and set her mind. "I will do as you ask, Peter. I pray you are right that this war will end soon." Fear washed over her and she said no more.

*

June 26, 1863

Elizabeth had been tending to the graves, as she did every morning, when she spotted them. She stepped to the fence that separated the cemetery from town and grabbed the metal rungs as the men in gray and butternut raced through town. They were shouting and shooting. Breaking into her neighbors' homes, forcing them into the streets. Riding their horses over fences and through yards and causing an uproar everywhere.

She stood frozen, her heart thundering in her ears as the men in gray terrorized Gettysburg's residents. She was more afraid than she'd ever been. For herself, the unborn babe she carried, and her three young boys.

She started to shake and gripped the fence for support. Darkness began to blot out the light. She gulped in air. It did no good and she collapsed into the soft grass.

She had no idea how long she lay there before she woke. When she did, all she could think about were her children, her mother and father. She turned in the direction of her home and saw that soldiers were headed that way.

In her sixth month with the stork, she dragged herself to her feet. Peter had come home on leave just after Christmas and three months later, Elizabeth realized she was expecting another child. Hopefully, a girl this time.

Once she was steady, she hurried as quickly as she could toward home. There, her mother was looking after the boys while she tended to her duties.

Fear for her family gave her the strength to put one foot in front of the other. Near the house, she jerked to an abrupt halt as several Confederate soldiers entered her front door.

She summoned every ounce of courage she possessed and charged inside in time to hear, "Give us food, woman." The man who had given Elizabeth's mother the order looked as thin as a scarecrow. So did the men with him.

Catherine stood in front of them, wide-eyed and shaking her head.

Elizabeth knew her mother had understood little, if any, of what the man said. Even though they'd been in America for over six years, neither her mother nor her father had worked at learning the new language. They still spoke only German.

Her mother stood rooted to the floor, staring at the soldier, her lips pinched, her chest heaving with fright.

"Didn't you hear me? Get moving," he shouted. "We want food."

Elizabeth cleared her throat and stepped further inside. "May I help you gentlemen?" she asked as calmly and cordially as she could.

The five men whirled toward her. Their eyes widened with surprise when they noticed her condition.

"We come for food, Ma'am," the soldier who had made the initial demand said.

Panic skittered up and down Elizabeth's spine as she spoke quickly in German to her mother. With several quick nods, Catherine Masser turned and hurried into the kitchen.

The children cried and shrieked for their mother from the other room. Although Elizabeth tried to mask her fear, the sound of her frightened children must have shown on her face.

The same soldier who had given the order for food swiped off his hat and, in a calm tone said, "Don't be afraid. We won't hurt you or your family." He paused then added, "We only want food."

Elizabeth nodded several times. "My mother shall prepare you a good meal. But she speaks no English." She waited for the man to acknowledge what she'd said then added, "May I go to my children? They are afraid."

"Of course." The soldier lifted his arm for her to leave the room.

She went to her boys and tried to soothe their fears. They were only seven, five and two, but the older boys understood well enough the men in their home had not been invited and did not mean well.

"Are they going to hurt us?" Frederick, the oldest, asked his mother, his voice a squeak.

"The man said they would not. They are hungry and only want food. Once their bellies are full, they will leave us alone." She hugged each of her children. "Frederick, watch over George and John. I must help your Grossmutter prepare food for them."

She left her children and went to help her mother.

When the two women brought out the food, the men filled their plates and went out into the cemetery to eat under a tree.

"They will leave when the food is gone," Elizabeth told her mother.

"Ja." Catherine nodded nervously. Tears gathered in her eyes.

Elizabeth hugged her and asked, "Where is Papa?"

"He was in our home. He must have hidden when the soldiers came. I saw some go inside, but they did not bring your papa out with them when they came here."

Elizabeth feared for her father, but couldn't go to him until the soldiers were gone. She went to the open window overlooking where the soldiers ate and joked. A man on horseback came upon them. He led a saddled yet riderless horse behind him.

"Where did you get that?" one of the lounging soldiers asked.

The rider drew his back up straight. "I killed the owner, a Union soldier."

Elizabeth slapped her hand over her mouth to keep from gasping out loud.

"Yes, the Blue Belly shot at me," he continued. "But did not hit me. I shot at him, blowed him down like nothing, and took his mount. He's lying down the pike."

Elizabeth felt her stomach flip. A man was dead and these...these soldiers joked about it! It was all she could do to keep the sourness in her belly from coming up.

The men in gray finished their meals and returned the dirty crockery to Elizabeth and Catherine. They even thanked them for the food before they mounted and left.

As soon as they were gone, Elizabeth ran to her parents' home. "Papa! Papa!" she screamed when she charged through the door.

John Masser stepped into the room behind them. His daughter fell into his arms.

"How did they not find you?" Elizabeth asked.

"I saw them coming. I sneaked around to the cellar and threw the bolt. It is a thick door and they could not get it open. I told them I was an old man and they had no fear of me. They finally left me alone."

"Oh, Papa, we were so scared." Elizabeth hugged him tightly, and sobbed with relief.

"Perhaps now they will leave us alone," her father said.

"Perhaps." Elizabeth wasn't so sure.

*

July 1, 1863 – First day of fighting at Gettysburg

Elizabeth jerked to a halt in front of the second-floor window that overlooked the cemetery and town. It had been several days since the Confederates left Gettysburg, and she hoped never to see them again. Now it was men in blue coming down Baltimore Street into town.

She kneaded her back, aching from the extra weight of the babe. The Federals came closer. "Dear Lord," she whispered. "Not again."

George called her from the other room. She left the window to tend to her middle son, along with all the other duties that couldn't be left undone. However, she returned to the window many times throughout the morning to observe the movements of the soldiers.

To her horror, as the day progressed Confederates appeared behind the Federals. By that afternoon, the men in gray were forcing the men in blue through town toward Cemetery Hill—and her home. To her dismay, a Union artillery force took up position on the hill across from the gatehouse.

Afraid for her family, she brought her parents to her residence. "We must stay together."

Shortly afterward there was a knock on the door. When she answered it, a blue-clad soldier swept his hat across his waist and bowed. "Madam. I am here at

General Howard's request. I seek to find a local man to assist in acquainting us with the layout of the town." He turned to her father, standing beside Elizabeth. "Might you be that man, Sir?"

Elizabeth's father looked askance at her. "I am sorry, Sir. My father does not understand. He does not speak English."

The soldier seemed distressed by Elizabeth's news. "Perhaps there is another man in the household that can do the task?"

Elizabeth shook her head. "There is only my father, mother and my children here. And me, of course." She thought a moment then added, "My husband is fighting with the 138th Pennsylvania Infantry, but I can guide you. I am not afraid."

"You, Ma'am?" He studied her protruding form and seemed perplexed by her proposal. "I could not."

"I speak English and know the layout of the town well. My parents can remain with my children. I shall go."

The man pondered a few moments then cocked his head and said, "Come on then."

Elizabeth told her parents what he was about and what she intended to do. They argued, but she was strong-willed and won in the end. "Take care of the boys. I shall return shortly. This man will not harm me. He will only be grateful, and grateful is a good thing right now."

When she turned around, the man stepped aside, allowing her to exit. He met her outside.

Elizabeth led the way through fields of flax, oats, and wheat. At one point in their journey, they came upon a troop of men who became agitated by her presence.

"What is a woman doing here?" one blue-clad man asked none too kindly.

"She is helping me learn the layout of this town," the aide told him. "At General Howard's request," he added, quieting the men's concerns.

They were quickly on their way. Elizabeth pointed out the York, Harrisburg, and Hunterstown Roads before the aide escorted her safely home.

Elizabeth explained again to her parents what she had been requested to do.

"You have done a good thing," her father told her. "Perhaps the Federals shall remember it another time."

Several hours later the family was beginning preparations for a sparse evening meal, when another knock drew Elizabeth's attention. She pulled open the door and gasped at the three Union generals standing on her doorstep.

All three men swept off their hats and bowed. One stepped forward.

"Madam, I am General Howard. I understand I am indebted to you for your assistance earlier." He turned to the men on either side of him. "These are Generals Slocum and Sickles."

The officers nodded.

Elizabeth curtsied and lowered her chin in acknowledgement.

General Howard continued. "I am afraid I must impose upon your good nature once again, Mrs...?"

"Thorn."

"Mrs. Thorn. I must ask you to accommodate my fellow officers and I with a meal."

Elizabeth took a deep breath. The Confederates had wiped out most of their supply pantry when they'd ridden through four days ago. But she was prideful and wouldn't let these important men go away hungry.

"The Confederates left us little when they came through here. I have no bread, but I shall bake some cakes and do my best to make a decent meal for you gentlemen."

"That is all we can ask, Madam," General Howard said with another bow.

Once inside, she pointed the three men to chairs in the front room then went to prepare what she could for them.

At the table an hour later, the three Thorn boys watched General Howard closely. With great animation he explained how he'd lost his arm at the Battle of Seven Pines a year earlier. Enthralled, the boys studied his empty arm sleeve as it flapped, their eyes growing wider and wider as the general continued his story. Little John, the youngest at almost three, pointed and giggled numerous times.

It was a humble meal, a few corn cakes and little meat, but it was food and the men were happy to get it.

As the officers prepared to leave, Howard took Elizabeth aside. "There will be hard fighting tomorrow. I urge you to take to your cellar for safety." He turned to leave then stopped and shook his head. "No. That is not good advice. You must leave this house now and get as far away as possible. Take nothing but the children and go."

"You want us to leave now?" The words stuck in her throat.

"Yes. For the safety of your family."

Elizabeth didn't doubt the general knew what he was talking about. There were, after all, big guns positioned across from her home and men from both armies nearby.

After the generals left, she gathered her parents and children and a few necessary items and hurried onto the Baltimore Pike, a short distance from the gatehouse.

On the outskirts south of town, with young John in her arms, she spotted a house to stop at for the night. However, when they reached it, dozens of Union soldiers had already found the same home in which to rest before the coming battle.

Stumbling over rows of prostrate men, Elizabeth found a place for her family to sleep. But sleep didn't come. Her stomach growled without cease. She'd managed a meal for the generals, but hadn't eaten a bite all day. As the night wore on, she began to feel ill.

"I must find food," she whispered to her father.

"There is nothing here. The soldiers have taken whatever this family had." He hesitated then said, "I shall go back to the gatehouse and gather what I can find. And anything else that may be of help to us."

Elizabeth shook her head. "What if you come upon soldiers? You can't speak to them. I shall go with you."

"You cannot. It is not good for you or the babe."

"None of this is good for the babe, or me, or my children, but I must have food. I am unwell because I am so hungry."

"Very well. Come." Her father stood and offered her his hand. "Catherine, watch over the boys," he told his wife. "We go for supplies. Elizabeth must have food and there is none here."

Tears pooled in Catherine Masser's eyes. "You must come back to me. Both of you. Be careful," she said sternly. She kissed her husband and daughter then took John in her arms and cradled the small boy to her chest.

Elizabeth and her father wended their way through the men strewn about the floor. She jerked to a halt when someone called to her. When she looked around, a soldier beckoned her.

He sat up and waited as she strode in his direction. When she reached him, he handed her a picture of three little boys. "These are my sons," he said in a gruff voice. "They're just like yours." He looked up through watery eyes. "Might you consider allowing your boys to sleep near me? I miss mine something terrible. If yours were close it would help ease my pain. The littlest one nearest to me, perhaps?"

Elizabeth wanted to weep from the sadness she saw in his eyes and the pain she heard in the homesick soldier's voice. She nodded, then turned to her father. She told him what she meant to do and, with no argument from him, they went back to her children. Her father gathered Frederick in his arms, while Elizabeth explained to her mother.

With a sad look at the hopeful soldier, Catherine relinquished her hold on John and put him in Elizabeth's outstretched arms.

By the time Elizabeth reached the soldier with her small burden, her father was already returning with George, placing the sleeping child near the grateful man. Catherine followed them and positioned herself near her grandchildren, watching.

Elizabeth almost wept with the relief and joy she saw in the young soldier's eyes.

Once the still-slumbering children were resettled, Elizabeth and her father left to gather whatever they could before tomorrow's battle. One way or another, it was going to be a long night.

*

After Midnight, July 2, 1863

Elizabeth stumbled and almost fell when they were close enough to see her home and what it looked like. Federals swarmed around it. All the windows had been shot out and men lay in the yard outside. Some cried in pain. Some begged for water, others for their mothers.

"I will check the pigs." Her father slipped away toward the back of the residence where the pen was located. Elizabeth waited, tears sliding down her cheeks as she studied the destruction of her home and the pitiful men around it.

Her father returned a few minutes later, shaking his head. "The pigs are gone."

Elizabeth didn't think it possible, but her shoulders slumped lower. "Perhaps we can get into the cellar to see if anything has been left there." She started toward the outside entrance. As she drew closer, she stopped. Men were going in and out carrying litters, some with wounded and some dead.

She waited until the soldiers going up and down stopped and, holding her breath, tip-toed down the stairs. What greeted her made her want to retch. Injured men lay about, some on featherbeds she recognized as hers, others on the dirt floor. Many begged to see their loved ones one last time before meeting their maker.

She gave those she could a ladle of water before seeking the chests that held all her worldly belongings. She lifted the lid of one, then the other. Both were empty. She went to the shelves where her few canned goods had been stored and stared at the emptiness. Her heart as vacant as the shelves, she turned to her father who had followed her in. "We should not tarry. There is nothing for us here. Come. Let us go."

As she headed toward the exit, she spied her mother's shawl on a peg beside the door. She grabbed it, wrapped it around her shoulders, and headed up the stairs, her heart heavy, her fear great.

Elizabeth and her father returned to the farmhouse where her mother and children slept. She plucked John from beside the slumbering soldier and awakened the other two boys. Her father woke his wife so they could begin another trek to find food. There was nothing for them here. They had to go farther from town if they wanted to find sustenance. Elizabeth prayed she would manage to stay upright until they found something to fill her empty belly.

*

The Masser/Thorn family left the crowded farmhouse behind and walked farther up the Baltimore Pike. As the sun began to rise, Elizabeth saw the outline of a farmhouse on the horizon.

"That is Henry Beitler's homestead over there." She pointed. "We've met several times at the mercantile in town and he was very kind to me. He was born here, but his family is from the old country. In one of our conversations, he told me his family farm was off the Baltimore Pike. He also said if I ever needed help while Peter was away, that I could call on him. That is where we must go." She started forward. "He will help us."

Before they reached the farm, the sounds of battle erupted from behind them.

Elizabeth jumped at the first explosion of artillery. She whirled toward where her home stood. Fear streaked up her spine, when she recalled the Union cannon standing across from her home.

Would there be a home for them to go back to? Would her family be left to wander the streets of Gettysburg, begging for scraps to sustain them? She pushed the unwanted thoughts from her mind. All they could do was survive today. Then tomorrow. Then the next.

They arrived at the Beitler farm to find several Union commands had taken over the home. Elizabeth did not fear the Union army. She turned to her parents, handed John to her mother and said, "I am going to see if I can get food."

Before her parents could protest, she strode to the front door and knocked. It was opened by a soldier who eyed her with surprise at such an early hour.

"What can I do for you, Madam?"

"I am looking for Mr. Henry Beitler. Is he here?" Her heart thumped and she clasped her hands in front of her to keep them from shaking. She needed food and she needed it now.

He tipped his hat. "The house was empty when we arrived, Ma'am." He swept his hand in front of her. "Please. Come in."

Elizabeth stepped inside. She felt light-headed and nearly swooned.

The soldier took her elbow and guided her to a chair.

"You look pale, Ma'am. Sit there a minute and catch your breath."

Elizabeth swallowed. "It's not rest I need, Sir. I have not eaten in nearly twenty-four hours." Now was the time for repayment of her kindness to the generals. "Your generals Howard, Slocum, and Sickles came to my home yesterday and I fed them. In the havoc that arrived with them, I did not eat and find myself feeling very unwell because of it." She took a deep breath. "My family is waiting outside. My mother, father and my three small children. Pray, might we get a meal?"

A very important-looking man with fringed epaulets on his uniformed shoulders and his hands locked behind him stepped into the front room. "Do whatever you can to assist this woman and her family." He strode closer and put out his hand. "I am General Alfred Pleasanton at your service, Madam. Whatever we can do to ease your suffering, we shall endeavor to do so."

Another general! So far, they had all been kind and this one appeared to be the same. Elizabeth relaxed as the aide hurried from the room to do the general's bidding.

Elizabeth shook the general's hand. "I am Elizabeth Thorn, Sir."

"Hmmm, the name sounds familiar."

"Sir? How could it?" Elizabeth began to shake again.

"Calm yourself, Madam. I was advised by General Howard that a young woman, in your condition, assisted him yesterday in an assessment of the town. Might I presume that was you?"

Elizabeth nodded. "It was."

"The general was quite impressed with your courage and willingness to provide aid."

Her heart slowed and she began to breathe normally again. "It was the least I could do to help."

"And in return, we shall give you and your family food and shelter away from the fighting."

"Thank you, Sir. That is so very kind."

Pleasanton waved his hand. "I admire your strength and courage. I shall do whatever I can to assist you and your family."

The aide returned with a tray of food.

"Go. Bring your family inside and eat," the general told her.

Elizabeth hurried outside, explained what had happened. She led her family back into the house where they ate until they were sated. The boys chattered like magpies with the friendly aide.

Once the meal was completed, the aide waived his hand toward the divan and several chairs. "Please, be comfortable."

Elizabeth stretched out, her children beside her and Little John on her chest. It wasn't long before she slept.

When she woke, afternoon sun streaked in through the windows. She stood and stretched, happy to have her belly full and her family safe.

It was then she heard it. The cries of wounded men coming from the wagon shed near the house. The sound of their agony tore through her.

"I shall go to them and do whatever I can to ease their suffering," she told her parents. "Watch the boys."

Before her parents could argue, she fled the house toward the shed. The smell that hit her when she entered made her afraid she would lose the food she'd recently eaten. The stench of blood, suffering, and death, flooded through her. The sight of a pile of discarded limbs and bloody rags made her gag.

Men in blue uniforms lay about the floor on blankets, cots, and in the straw. In every frightened, bloodied face she saw her husband. She prayed that if he were injured somewhere, a kind woman would be there to help him in his time of need.

She stood rooted to the ground for several minutes before reminding herself she was there to help. She stiffened her back, steeled herself against the sights, sounds, and smells around her, and went to work.

With the echo of battle in the distance, Elizabeth tended the wounded throughout the rest of the day and into the night. Only when her father brought food did she cease her ministrations long enough to eat and drink before she continued her mission of mercy.

*

July 3, 1863

It was after midnight. Elizabeth rubbed her distended belly and worried if her earlier lack of food might affect her unborn child. Was the babe safe in her womb from the backbreaking work? Her spine was so sore from the extra weight she carried she thought it would snap in half. Her eyes so heavy she thought if given the chance, she could sleep standing up.

The weakness in her legs finally forced her to go inside the house. She collapsed on the divan, but slept little from her physical discomfort and worry, even though the house was ringed by soldiers and her family slept close by.

When she wakened the next morning after a fitful sleep, she ate enough to break her fast then went out as quickly as her aching body allowed to continue her work in the shed. Her dress was stained with the blood of those souls she'd helped, but her heart was filled with the knowledge she'd done all she could to ease their suffering—or give them peace on their way to meet God.

It was toward the noon hour when a rider came in. Word passed quickly through the ranks that a young woman in town had been killed earlier that morning by a stray bullet.

Elizabeth was nearly inconsolable when she learned her friend, Jennie Wade, was the young woman killed. She cried out like a wounded animal and grabbed a chair to keep from falling.

"We were...we were friends," she told the soldier guiding her to a chair. "What happened?" she managed to ask through the lump of pain in her throat.

"A bullet passed through the outer door of her sister's home where she'd been staying. Then it went through the door that separated the kitchen from the front room." He looked away, as though unwilling to tell her the rest.

"Please, Sir, go on."

He grimaced and nodded. "She was making biscuits for our men on Cemetery Hill. The bullet struck her in the back where she stood." He swallowed. "Be assured, it was quick and she did not suffer."

Heartbroken, Elizabeth thanked the man and went back to her work, helping where she could, offering solace when needed.

It was what Jennie would have done.

As the 3rd day of July progressed, so did the sound of combat. Artillery exploded. Gunfire popped. The bellow of men charging into battle echoed across the usually quiet fields. A smoky, gray haze hung over the town, blocking out the sun.

Toward night, the sounds faded. The shouts of men surging forward fell silent. With her charges resting comfortably, Elizabeth went to the house and did what Jennie had been doing at her death. She made bread to feed the hungry soldiers and civilians who had come to the house seeking help, just as she and her family had.

She was exhausted, but it was an exhaustion like nothing she'd ever felt before. She was heartbroken about her friend and worn out, to be sure. Her back, neck and legs ached, but she felt compelled to continue doing whatever she could to help those in need.

July 4th, Independence Day, dawned silent save the crow of roosters. Elizabeth dared to hope the battle was done. It wasn't until word of the Union victory passed through the men, and that General Lee was already withdrawing his Confederates toward Virginia, did she believe it was finally over.

But the men who were wounded too badly to travel remained at the Beitler home. They still needed Elizabeth's help. And she intended to give it.

She worked day and night caring for those men. It was a labor she could not be diverted from, while her parents looked after her children. Perhaps her boys didn't understand her absence now, but someday she hoped they would be proud of what she'd done. If she helped comfort or save one life in the aftermath of this horrific battle, it was well-worth her discomfort and toil.

It was Tuesday, July 7th, when Elizabeth told her mother and father, "It's time to go home. The last of the wounded were taken away at first light this morning."

They collected their few belongings and headed out the door, each adult clutching one of the children's hands in theirs. Elizabeth's step was quick in her impatience to get home, although she feared what she would find.

*

Along the road the little troupe met Mr. McConaughy, the president of the cemetery Elizabeth worked for.

"Hurry on home," he told her. "There is more work than you are able to do." He shook his head sadly then rode on.

Images of what awaited them crowded Elizabeth's mind the rest of the way. When she reached the gatehouse, her worst thoughts couldn't compare with reality.

"Oh my," was all she could manage in her astonishment and dismay as she stared at the bodies of dozens of men and horses that lay outside the cemetery. How in the Lord's name could she bury them all? In her condition? In the oppressive heat? Her father held her upright when her knees threatened to buckle.

The foul stench of death smacked her in the face, clung to her skin, crawled up her nose, made her eyes pool and leak onto her cheeks. She shivered, despite the high temperature, and lifted her skirt to her face. She pressed the material around her nose in an effort to blot out the putrid smell. It didn't work.

The children coughed, complained of the smell, and cried. Her mother tore strips from her dress and petticoat then tied them around the boys' noses, choking all the while until she covered her own face. Elizabeth's father pinched his nose. His eyes watered.

"In all the years I have worked at the cemetery, I have never smelled anything so foul." Elizabeth's words were muffled through the material covering her face.

"Nor have I," her father managed.

Elizabeth studied the carnage when they reached her home. Besides the bodies of horses and men left outside her home, the gatehouse had been severely damaged. Not only was every window broken, as she'd witnessed the night she and her father went back in search of food, several of the frames had been knocked out as well.

When she mustered the courage to go inside, the devastation took her breath away. Her furniture was strewn about, much of it in pieces. Glass lay below the shattered windows. The floors were scuffed and covered with mud and blood.

Tears streamed down Elizabeth's face. She recalled the featherbeds she'd seen in the cellar the last time she'd been down there and headed outside and around the house. When she descended the stairs and saw the condition of the cellar, a fierce anger swept over her.

"Never have I seen such disregard for property in my life," she railed to no one. With her lumbering bulk, she grabbed the end of one of the beds and pulled it up the stairs, her anger so great she needed no help. One at a time she dragged them up and dropped them on the ground.

When a rider came up behind her, she whirled on him. Noting he was an officer she voiced her discontent. "Do you see what your army did?" She waved at the featherbeds. "Shall I ever get any pay for my things spoiled like this?"

He studied the beds then studied her. "No," he said with no regret and rode on.

Deflated, she watched him ride away, shaking her head as she walked to her parents' house. She found it in better condition than hers.

Elizabeth went to find some linens in her parents' house. Most were now rags but could be used to help mask the foul stench of the dead. She tore several pieces and tied them around her nose and mouth.

"I must see to cleaning the bedding so the children have someplace to sleep with a little comfort. There will be no recompense to replace them, so we must make the best with what remains," she said aloud to the empty room.

Step by agonizing step, Elizabeth dragged the beds to the pump and began to scrub. Soon, several ladies who lived nearby, out surveying the damage left behind after the battle, joined her. In the brutal heat, sweat pouring down their faces, they scoured until their hands bled and the beds showed little signs of blood or mud.

In the midst of Elizabeth's scrubbing, David McConaughy rode up.

He dismounted, surveyed the area, then said, "Mrs. Thorn, you are to begin burial of those bodies left outside the cemetery. Commence preparing lots facing East Cemetery and Culp's Hill as fast as you can."

"East Cemetery?" Elizabeth nearly shouted. "The rockiest soil in the cemetery is there." She shook her head and stared at the man. "I am but one woman and three months shy of giving birth to another child. Who is to help me in this task?"

McConaughy waved at two soldiers still mounted behind him. They got off and walked to Elizabeth. "These men will remain to assist you."

"Two men?" She couldn't believe it. A small army was needed to bury all these men. "There are dozens to be buried. Perhaps a hundred or more. Their bodies are already bloating and bursting in the heat. And do not forget the horses. What am I to do with them?" Her heart thundered in her chest she was so enraged that he would lay such a difficult task upon her.

"You must do the best you can. I shall go into town and seek volunteers. That is all I can do." He remounted. "Begin immediately. It cannot wait."

Elizabeth nearly harumphed in his face as he looked down on her. *There is so much more you could do. Like come down from that high horse and help with the burying yourself! But, no, you are above that.*

Before she could voice her thoughts, he whirled his horse around and rode away.

Elizabeth turned to the two men who had remained behind. Both were pale and looked as though they would retch at any moment.

She bent over, tore off two long strips from her underskirt, and handed one to each man. "Tie this around your nose and mouth. It doesn't stop the smell, but it helps."

The two soldiers hurried to tie off the strips then followed Elizabeth to the tool shed where she handed them each a shovel. After explaining where the graves needed to be dug, the men set off across the cemetery.

Elizabeth's father built a litter to transport the dead from the field to the graves. It was gruesome work, but there was no other way for it to be done. Once the litter was complete, the soldiers' horses were employed to move the bodies to the graves.

Elizabeth knew these two men wouldn't last long when the first body arrived at the graves they'd dug. Both soldiers' eyes bulged when they saw the condition of the remains. One, then the other, leaned over and lost their stomachs.

It was all Elizabeth could do to keep from losing hers, between the smell of the dead and their retching.

The day wore on, the heat stifling, the odor overpowering. She found a small bottle of perfume that hadn't been destroyed and sprinkled generous amounts on hers, her father's, and the soldiers' makeshift masks. It gave them enough relief to continue working another two days before the soldiers grew sick.

"I can't go on," the one named Matthew said.

The other, Jacob, nodded, his face as pale as parchment paper.

Matthew swallowed hard. "We didn't sign up for this. The perfume isn't working anymore. I can't do it another day."

"You can't go. What am I to do with the bodies still left to be buried?" She looked down at her swelling belly. "Am I to dig the graves myself? Or my elderly father? You can't leave now. How are we to finish our task?"

"We'll leave one of the horses to pull the litter," Matthew said. "We just can't stay any longer. That's all there is to it."

Matthew and Jacob strode away, leaving Elizabeth with an even more daunting task than she'd begun with. Perhaps forty men had been buried. Who would help her with the dozens that were left?

Elizabeth's father stepped beside her and rested his hand on the small of her back. "We shall do it. Mama will care for the boys and we shall get it done. I am an old man but not so feeble I cannot dig a few graves."

"A few graves, Papa? There are dozens more to be dug."

He touched her cheek. "And we shall do it."

She stared at her father, squared her shoulders, and set her mind to the task. If he was willing, so was she. "Very well." She thought of the men awaiting burial. "Each one of those men is someone's brother or father or son. They shall have a decent final resting place and the respect they deserve."

Elizabeth set to work. She marked off the graves and her father dug. For weeks they worked in the blistering sun and heat to get the graves marked, dug, and filled. Several men from town finally came to help, but the foul smell drove them away. Two became deathly ill.

It had been six weeks since the battle ended and the undertaking of burying the dead had begun. Wearing the same dress she had on when they began, Elizabeth used the back of her hand to push her sweaty hair off her forehead. "That was the last one," she told her father. "We have succeeded."

John Masser, who had lost much weight in the completion of their task, nodded. "We have."

Elizabeth pulled the mask below her nose. She strode from the last grave and sniffed the air. For the first time in weeks the smell of death didn't ride the wind. Only her own stench assaulted her nose.

She gazed out over where the men and horses had lain. "Thank God someone dragged the horses away. I do not know who it was, but I am thankful. I could not have borne such an undertaking."

Her father put his arm around her shoulders. "Come. It is time to forget all that has happened and go home."

"Yes, it is time to go home. But I shall never forget."

Afterword

After six weeks of burying the dead, Elizabeth, seven months pregnant by that time, and her father, sixty-three years old, had buried one hundred and five souls. One report states they were all soldiers ("*History of American Women*"). Another states ninety-one soldiers were buried ("*Those Were Hard Days*"). Another says there were ninety-one soldiers and fourteen civilians buried ("*America Comes Alive!*"). However, other sources say the **only civilian** casualty at Gettysburg was Jennie Wade ("*Jennie Wade of Gettysburg: The Complete Story of the Only Civilian Killed During the Battle of Gettysburg*" Cindy L. Small, Gettysburg Publishing.)

On November 1, 1863, Elizabeth gave birth to a little girl she named Rose Meade, in honor of General George Meade who commanded the Union Army of the Potomac. Rose was a sickly child and lived only fourteen years.

Elizabeth ran the cemetery until Peter returned home after Appomattox in 1865. The family lived at Evergreen Cemetery as caretakers until 1874.

In 1905, Elizabeth wrote a post-war reminiscence, which is considered to be one of the best-known civilian accounts of the Battle at Gettysburg.

Elizabeth's parents lived with her and Peter the rest of their lives. John Masser died in July of 1869, Catherine in 1890. Five more children were born to Peter and Elizabeth after the battle.

In 1874 Peter gave up his position as caretaker of the cemetery and purchased a nearby farm. He died in 1907 at age 82. Elizabeth died several months later at the age of 74. Both are buried at the Evergreen Cemetery.

In 2002, the Women's Memorial was dedicated to the many women who served during that terrible conflict. The monument (pictured earlier) depicts an expectant Elizabeth Thorn.

References

Taken from a summary on the internet at: www.thegettysburgexperience.com/elizabeththorn from the book ELIZABETH THORN: "Those Were Hard Days" by Diana Loski

History of American Women at:
www.womenhistoryblog.com/2007/05/elizabeth-thorn.html

America Comes Alive! at:
https://americacomesalive.com/elizabeth-thorn-1832-1907-six-months-pregnant-burying-dead-gettysburg/

What Made Boys Become Guerillas in the "War of Northern Aggression?"

May 23, 1863

Fifteen-year-old Jesse James jerked hard on the mule's reins. The plow in front of him shuddered to a halt, the animal flinging its head back and forth against the abrupt stop.

His body stiff with uncertainty, Jesse stared at the Union militia boys riding into the yard of his family farm. Why had they come? Was it to take their home because they were loyal to the south? Or to find his older brother Frank, who rode with Quantrill's guerillas?

Frank wasn't here.

Jesse slipped the reins over his neck. He dropped them to the ground and ran for the house, his heart thrumming a wild beat in his chest.

"I know they're somewhere nearby," a man shouted as Jesse drew close. "Find them!" The men scattered.

Jesse came to a skidding stop beside his four-months pregnant mother, Zerelda. She stood beside his stepfather, Reuben Samuel, the man his brothers and sisters called Pappy. His two-year-old brother, J.T., and sister Sarah, five, peeked out from behind the skirts of his fourteen-year-old sister, Susan. Their frightened whimpering incited his rage further.

"Frank's not here," Pappy said in a controlled tone.

Hands on her generous hips, her face hard and set, Jesse's mother stomped forward. "No, he is not!

None of them boys are. Now git an' leave us plain folk to our own business."

Jesse sucked in a deep breath to refill his depleted lungs. He studied the men as they rejoined the others, shaking their heads in defeat. He was shocked to see their neighbor, Brantley Bond, among them. The man had served with Frank in the Confederacy's Missouri State Guard at the start of the war. Jesse's eyes widened further when he noticed Alvis Dagley, another neighbor, amongst the intruders.

The man in charge stepped closer to Jesse's folks, his nose inches from Pappy's. "If they're not here, they're close. You're going to tell me where."

Jesse squared his shoulders and took a step forward. He raised his chin and tried to look older and more confident than he was. "They said he ain't here and he ain't!"

The leader flicked his gaze toward two of his men. They strode to Jesse and grabbed him by the arms.

"Let go a me." Jesse struggled against the bigger, stronger men. "Let me go!" he screamed as he was dragged away.

Susan charged after them. She was batted away like a gnat and fell in the dirt crying. J.T. and Sarah screeched from where their sister had left them huddled together in front of the porch.

Further enraged, Jesse struggled harder, but was helpless against the strength of the two men.

He wasn't dragged far before he was released and pain exploded from a fist in his jaw. He cradled his face and went to his knees. Touched the tender spot where blood trickled from a split lip.

"Where's your brother?" one man shouted.

Jesse looked up and glared but remained mute.

A fist in his stomach sent him sprawling on the ground. He rolled into a ball, gasping for breath.

"I asked you a question, boy. Where's your brother and those no-accounts he rides with?"

Jesse remained silent, although he knew doing so would invoke their wrath further. But he wouldn't tell. Not even if he knew.

They pulled him to his feet and tore his shirt away. One man pinned his arms behind him, while the other laid the flat side of a saber across his bare chest. He jerked upright and cried out with each strike, the pain more than he'd ever felt before in his life.

Jesse kicked and tried to pull free of the two men, but he was out-numbered and out-manned. Blow after blow from fists, feet and saber left him bloodied and short of breath before he was abandoned in a heap on the hard-packed earth.

Straddled over Jesse's limp body one man said, "This young pup isn't so high and mighty now."

"Must not know where that brother of his is," the other said. "If he did, he'd have told us by now." There was a pause then he chuckled. "It doesn't matter one way or the other. He's a Reb and got what he deserves."

With a last kick to his ribs, the men strode away laughing.

Barely able to lift his head, Jesse watched in horror as Bond and Dagley put a rope around Pappy's neck, then threw the other end over a thick tree branch. Jesse tried to gain his feet, but fell back with a groan.

All he could do was watch.

His stepfather was slowly hoisted in the air until his feet no longer touched the ground. He kicked. Clawed at the rope. A gurgle was the only sound that came from his mouth. His eyes closed before he was dropped, gasping.

Jesse looked on, scratching at the dirt with his fingers. His rage was so great he would have killed every man there had he been able.

"Where are they?" the leader screamed at Pappy where he lay trying to catch his breath.

Jesse's mother shoved between them. "Stop. Stop this right now you miserable Yanks!" Her eyes flashed with undisguised hatred when she turned them on Bond and Dagley. "And you two. Traitors both of you. You're worse than a sow's belly draggin' in the dirt. We was neighbors!"

"Be still, woman," the leader shouted.

"How can I be still when you are hanging my husband?" she shrieked. She was dragged out of the way, her children wailing behind her.

"We came to get Frank and the boys he's riding with. And you're going to tell us where they are," the man in charge said to Pappy.

"What have they done that you're in such an all-fired rage to find them?" Jesse's stepfather asked, his voice like the croak of a toad.

The leader clenched the older man's chin between the fingers of his gloved right hand. "I'd bet my next pay voucher you already know." He looked up and scowled at Zerelda then thrust his chin toward Jesse. "I'd bet all of you know why we want him, but I'll tell you anyway. A few days ago, him and over a dozen men we believe ride with Quantrill, ambushed five Federal soldiers just outside Missouri City. Two of the soldiers got away. Another was shot three times, robbed and left for dead. But private Rapp, survived. And when those Bushwhackers found out he was still alive, they followed him to the Hardwick Hotel in Missouri City and shot him three more times." The soldier edged closer, grinned maliciously then snarled, "But he still isn't dead."

His grin disappeared when he continued, "The two officers, Captain Darius Sessions and Lieutenant Louis Grafenstein, were murdered like dogs. Both were shot in the head, more than once, along with the dozens of other bullets in their bodies." The man gritted his teeth then added, "And if that wasn't enough killing and robbing to satisfy them, they attacked Plattsburg the next day."

When Jesse had heard the news about the raid a couple of days ago while he was in Liberty, he'd applauded. Quantrill's boys had made the Federals pay for arresting Mrs. Moses McCoy, who'd said she'd "aided" Bushwhackers by feeding them. But it was well-known she fed *any* man who was hungry, regardless of his uniform.

However, it was likely the other charge against her was what got her arrested. The one that stated she'd made uniforms for Confederate recruits. Well, her husband was, after all, a Confederate recruiter. It stood to reason they would watch her to get to him. They knew he'd been to see her that same day, but she wouldn't tell where he went.

She was arrested, taken from her children, and paraded through Missouri City in her nightgown. After that humiliation, she was sent upriver to the Provost Marshall in St. Joseph. That was all Jesse knew about her arrest, except for the raid that followed.

On their way through here yesterday, Frank had told him he'd ridden with Moses McCoy, Lou's husband, and over a dozen other Quantrill men in retaliation. Frank had also confided it was his first real engagement as one of Quantrill's Bushwhackers.

Jesse's stomach tightened. He had a bad feeling these soldiers wouldn't give up their hunt for Frank and his companions until they were found.

"They aren't here I tell you," his stepfather cried out.

The man in charge stuck his face in Pappy's again. "We don't believe you." He waved his hand in a circle above his head. The rope tightened and Pappy was hoisted up again.

"Stop," Zerelda begged from where she stood, her arms gripped between two militia men.

Jesse's heart thundered like a hammer on an anvil, but he could do nothing. He was as weak as a babe. Every part of his body hurt.

Pappy was dropped again. Red faced, he gagged and coughed. He spit up blood and his eyes watered.

Bond leaned in close. "Unless you want to go up again, Dr. Samuel, I'd tell them what they want to know." His tone was almost pleading, as though he really didn't want to see his former neighbor's neck stretched again.

Jesse's stepfather shook his head and groaned. "I don't know where they are."

The leader waved his hand again and, for a third time, Jesse's stepfather was lifted off the ground. His eyes rolled and his mouth worked, but nothing came out. Finally, he was dropped.

As Jesse's stepfather fell to the ground, a rider pounded into the yard. He jumped from his horse and ran to Pappy. It was the Reverend William James, brother of Zerelda's first husband, Robert, who had died in California ministering to the prospectors searching for gold. The reverend pulled out a knife and cut the rope.

"We have more rope," the militia leader said with a glint in his eyes. "And the next time we stretch his neck, we'll leave him up there. To die." He waved for his men to restrain the Reverend James.

"You must stop this," James said, but gave no resistance when his arms were wrenched behind his back.

Pappy lifted his hand. "I'll tell you what...what you want...but I need water..." His head lolled to the side.

A ladle was put to his lips. He choked and coughed. More water spilled from his mouth than he swallowed. When he pushed the dipper away, he closed his eyes and said, "Check the woods to the north. If they're here, that's where they'll be."

Zerelda broke free and ran to Reuben, shouting curses at the soldiers. She dropped to her knees beside her husband, cradled his head in her bosom, and smoothed his forehead. When she looked up, Jesse imagined had this been an ancient story of witches and monsters, daggers of fire would have flown from her eyes.

He understood every unspoken word.

When Pappy stopped coughing and breathed normally again, as normally as he could with a nearly crushed windpipe, he was hauled like a sack of feed to his feet.

"What are you going to do with him?" Zerelda asked.

"What do you think we're gonna do? We're gonna shoot him." The man's eyes were filled with malice.

Jesse tried again to gain his feet, but only managed to stumble to his knees. He pounded the earth with what little strength he had, furious he could do nothing to stop his stepfather from being dragged away. His former neighbors mounted their horses with the others and followed. Jesse was left in the dirt. Zerelda, still giving the militia a tongue-lashing as they rode away with her husband, tried to follow but was restrained by her former brother-in-law.

"I have to stop them from hurting Reuben. I won't let them kill him without a fight." Her legs buckled and she fell to her knees. Her brother-in-law knelt beside her, and took her in his arms as she sobbed.

The children ran to their mother and wrapped their arms around her. Then, the only sound was the whimpering of a family mourning the uncertain fate of their loved ones.

*

Jesse slapped away the hands grabbing at him.

"Stop, Jesse. It's Ma."

Jesse stilled and opened his eyes. It took a moment for the fuzziness to disappear before her face came into focus. She studied him, her eyes soft. "You'll be fine now." She slid a wet cloth over his forehead and mouth. He jerked his head aside when it touched his busted lip.

"Where's Pappy?" he managed, his mouth and tongue twice their normal size.

Zerelda sniffed. "They took him out behind the house near to a quarter hour ago. Said they was gonna shoot him. But I ain't heard no shots. Maybe they're gonna leave him be." Jesse didn't mistake the hope in her voice.

Jesse's mother scooted to the side and his uncle came into view. "Come on, boy, let's git you inside."

Jesse was heaved to his feet at the same time several shots sounded from behind the house. He jerked his head up. "Did they shoot him, Ma? Did they shoot Pappy?" He winced from the pain that shot through his lips.

Zerelda stood silent, her back stiff as a post, her eyes toward where the shots had come from. Then her face hardened, her eyes narrowed, and her fists clenched. She turned to Susan. "Take the children inside." Her tone brooked no argument. She grabbed up her skirts and ran behind the house.

Jesse's uncle followed, hauling Jesse beside him. They found Zerelda staring into the woods to the north where Pappy told the militia Frank and the other guerillas would be. She stood, her body stiff, her hands crushing her skirt at her sides in her fists.

Finally able to stand on his own, Jesse stumbled to his mother.

"They musta took Reuben with 'em," she said when he stepped beside her. "To show 'em where Frank and the boys would be holed-up." Her breath hitched. "They musta found 'em."

"Frank and them boys are slick, Zerelda," William told her. "They wouldn't get caught unawares."

She turned eyes full of venom on him. "Does that mean Frank and the boys got away and they shot Reuben? Somebody was shootin'!"

"Now, Zerelda, let's don't git ahead of ourselves. We got no idea who was shootin' at who," William said.

"I'll find out, Ma." Jesse turned to run into the woods, but stopped when his mother called after him, "You can't. You ain't up to it." He whirled around when she added, "They already beat you half to death."

Jesse stiffened his spine. He sucked in a deep breath and let fury infuse strength through his young body. "I ain't dead and don't intend to be anytime soon. I'll find out where Pappy is, and Frank, if he's still here." He sprinted into the woods without giving his mother or uncle a chance to dispute his decision. Or see his pain.

Everything hurt. His face. His back. His legs and ribs. But he kept on. He had to know if Pappy and Frank were all right.

He was close to the clearing where he supposed his brother and the boys would have been. A place he and Frank had spent many hours climbing trees and gigging frogs in the creek nearby.

He dropped behind some bushes when he spotted the militia men wandering through what looked like an abandoned camp. They were checking the saddle bags and belongings left behind by the fugitives in their haste to escape. The soldiers kicked over cups. Cards left behind when attacked were flung in the air, the soldiers' frustration evident.

Jesse grinned, until he spotted Pappy checking the bodies of two men on the ground a short distance away. He hauled in a ragged breath. *Is one of them Frank? Are they dead?*

Pappy glanced up, toward where Jesse was hiding.

Jesse leaned out from behind the bushes far enough for his stepfather to see him and waved. When Pappy saw him, his eyes grew wide.

Jesse pointed at the bodies.

Pappy shook his head, silently telling his stepson neither man was his brother.

Jesse breathed again. He looked on, helpless, as the soldiers finished destroying the camp. They then tied his stepfather's hands behind his back, and helped him, none too gently, onto a horse. When the soldiers remounted, with Pappy in tow, they started not toward Liberty as Jesse had suspected they would, but for the James' house.

Still crouched behind the bushes, Jesse's heart felt as though it would explode as the militia headed back toward his home.

He crept deeper into the underbrush until the riders passed. When they were well away, rage gave him strength to ignore his injuries again and he followed.

Jesse was too late when he reached the house. His mother and Pappy were in a buckboard that was already leaving the yard. Jesse tried to run after them, but his uncle stopped him.

"Don't Jess. There's nothing we can do."

"Why are they taking Ma? What did she do except try to protect her husband and son? Where are they taking them?"

"Simmer down. They're taking her and Dr. Samuel to the Liberty jail." His uncle grabbed Jesse's upper arms and shook him. "There's nothing to be done right now. We have to wait."

"For what? Till they make an example out of Ma for not tellin' where Frank was? Or hang Pappy for real?"

"Your Ma is with child. They won't hurt her."

Jesse glared at his uncle then snorted. "Look what they already done, Uncle Will. They stretched Pappy's neck. Beat me senseless, and treated our womenfolk and the children like trash. I'd a never thought even dirty Yankees would do something like this, but here we are. I don't trust them worth a spit not to hurt Ma and Pappy."

"You're right. They're making an example of them," his uncle admitted. "Because they didn't cooperate and tell them where Frank was. They want folks to know it won't be tolerated."

"I hate Yankees. Hate 'em all!" Jesse shouted over his shoulder when he stormed into the house, nearly wrenching it off the hinges when he slammed it shut behind him.

*

Jesse waited for days for his parents to return. During that time, he cared for his younger brother and sisters. He also questioned everything he'd believed in before that fateful day.

On the porch of an evening while Susan was getting the children settled in their room for the night, he spoke with God. "If you are so benevolent, how could you let this happen? Any of it? The war? What happened here? Ma is a Godfearing woman. And Pappy, well, there is no better man." He held his hands above his head. "Why, God? Why? I believed in you. So much that I even considered following you like my pa and Uncle Will. But now…" His hands dropped to his sides. "Now all I feel is anger. Especially toward Mr. Bond and Mr. Dagley." He sucked in a deep breath before he said through gritted teeth, "They didn't even try to stop them militia boys from stretching Pappy's neck!"

At that moment, fifteen-year-old Jesse Woodson James knew he would never be the same person, or believe in the same things, again.

*

Early June, two weeks later

Jesse jerked upright when he heard a wagon coming up the lane. He pushed away from the table and said to Susan, "Take J.T. and Sarah in the back bedroom."

"Aw, Jesse, do we have to?" Sarah whined. "I don't wanna."

"Do as I say. There are riders comin' and I don't want any of you seen." He gave his sisters and brother a little push to send them on their way. "No sass now. Go on."

Sarah snatched the doll she'd been playing with from the table and followed Susan and J.T. into the other room.

Minutes later his mother called out, "It's all right. It's Ma and Pappy."

Jesse's heart quickened. He ran from the house to greet his mother and stepfather.

"Good riddance," the soldier driving the wagon shouted. He slapped the reins across the horse's backside to send the dray speeding away only moments after Pappy and Zerelda had stepped off.

"Ma! Pappy!" Jesse hugged his mother then his stepfather. "I'm so glad you're home. Tell me what happened."

Zerelda put up her hand. "First, where are my other children? Are they safe?"

Jesse yelled into the house. "Susan, bring J.T. and Sarah outside. Ma and Pappy are home!"

The children bounded through the door. Zerelda gathered them into her arms. She kissed them all over their faces. "Oh, my babies. I missed you. Mama's home now."

"And I'm glad of it, Ma." Jesse smiled for the first time in weeks.

"Let's go in the house." Zerelda entered the children clutched at her sides. Pappy followed, Jesse behind him. He noted his stepfather's silence and a strange, faraway look on his face.

"Let's sit down and I'll tell you about it." His mother patted Jesse's hand.

Zerelda sat at the table across from Reuben with Susan on one side of her and Jesse on the other. Sarah and J.T. played quietly on the floor nearby. She took Jesse's hand and began.

"That awful day they took me and Reuben to the Liberty jail."

"How did they treat you? In your delicate condition?" Jesse's rage began to swell again.

She squeezed his fingers. "I won't tell you it wasn't…difficult, but we survived. After Liberty, they took us to the Provost Marshall in St. Joe." She turned sad eyes to her husband. She reached for Reuben's hand with her free one. Her lips trembled when she turned back to Jesse. "We're lucky they didn't kill him, but…"

"But what, Ma?" Susan asked when her mother didn't finish the sentence.

Tears filled Zerelda's otherwise hard eyes. "He's not the same. Not like he used to be. The trip to St. Joe and the time he was there…did something to him. More than what was already done." Her tone had grown harsh.

Jesse's eyes snapped to his stepfather's and saw what he hadn't before. They were blank, as though he wasn't even in the same room. A chill passed over him and Jesse had to keep himself from screaming out his fury. Yet another reason for him to hate Yankees.

"He'll never be the same," Zerelda grit out.

Susan gasped.

Reuben's eyes suddenly cleared. His shoulders squared and, in a strong voice he said, "I may not be the man I was, but I thank the good Lord I'm not dead." The clarity in his eyes disappeared and they went blank again.

"The good Lord," Jesse said with a snarl. "What did He do that was so good for you that you'd be thankful for any part of what happened to you? Or Ma? Or me?" he challenged.

His mother squeezed Jesse's hand. "We won't speak on that right now."

Jesse could see she was holding her temper. He'd seen that temper enough in his lifetime to know when it was simmering.

"Reuben is tired now." She turned to her husband. "Let's find your bed."

As obedient as a puppy, he followed her into their room.

Jesse's hatred had grown so full inside him, he had to get out of there before he lost control. He jumped to his feet, shoved through the door, and ran behind the house. He screamed. Punched one tree then another until his knuckles bled and he could barely breathe.

His rage had been vented. It was by no means assuaged.

*

March or April, 1864

Jesse sat on the stoop outside the house. He lifted his face to the setting sun. They'd made it through the winter. It was a new year and spring was coming. But with the spring came the planting. It was backbreaking work and he was the only one left to do it with Frank gone and Pappy, well…not the same.

Jesse sighed. He'd spent the last year working the farm alone. Had even brought in a good tobacco crop late last summer. The hard work and knowledge that he'd done a good job should have lessened the pain and anxiety of what had happened to him and his family, but it didn't.

Each morning he woke with his gut coiled and mental images of Pappy swinging, thrashing and choking. The children crying, his mother trying to ease their fear and her temper, while Jesse clawed at the ground, unable to stop any of it.

Winter or summer, of a morning he threw off the covers soaked in sweat. Then, as the day progressed, he relived the events over and over.

Jesse's chin snapped up when he heard horses on the lane. He grabbed his gun, the one he kept tucked in his belt now, stood and waited.

Two strangers reined their horses to a stop in front of him. They were dressed in what he knew to be the garb of local guerillas. Their fancy embroidered shirts were crossed by ammo belts and gun holsters, their beards and hair long. Jesse knew their ilk. His brother was one of them.

He held the gun low but cocked and ready. "What're you boys about?" he asked. A twinge of doubt raced through him. Were they here to tell him something had happened to Frank?

Before Jesse could ask, the closest rider waved a gloved hand. "Kin I dismount without you raisin' that hog leg?"

"Depends. Why are you here?"

"We come to talk to you."

"About what?"

"About ridin' with us." He paused then added, "And Frank."

"Is Frank all right?" Jesse asked in a rush.

The man waved his hand again. "The gun?"

"Oh." Jesse un-cocked the pistol and shoved it into the front of his trousers.

The man dismounted and stepped toward him.

"Is Frank all right?" Jesse asked a second time.

"He's fine, but he's worried about his little brother."

"Who are you?"

"Fletch Taylor. I ride with Frank. Have since our raid in Missoura City last May." The man looked around. "Sun is settin'. Maybe we could put up in your barn for the night? We kin talk there." He lifted an eyebrow and waited for Jesse to answer.

Jesse turned toward the house where his mother was reading to the children in the back bedroom. And his stepfather, well, he didn't care much about anything these days.

Jesse stepped down from the porch. "This way." He led the two men to the barn where they unsaddled their horses. When they were settled Jesse sat down on an overturned bucket and asked, "Did Frank send you?"

"He's worried about his family, but especially about you." Taylor scrubbed at his bearded chin. "I kin tell you when he heard what happened last year with the militia, he was madder'n a wet hen. It was all we could do to keep him from coming here and tracking down whoever done it. We had to convince him he'd get hisself caught, or killed, if he did."

"So, he sent you to do…what?"

"Bring you back with us."

Excitement zinged through Jesse, until he thought about what he would leave behind. "What about my ma? And Pappy and the children? My stepfather ain't in his right mind anymore. Who will take care of them if I go?"

Fletch sniggered. "Frank tole us all about your ma. Said she ain't no witherin' rose and kin take care of herself, her children, and anybody else she needs to. Said you got a sister kin help with the young 'uns too."

Jesse smiled. If there was one thing he knew about Zerelda James, she was strong and determined. She'd made her boys strong. And Susan too.

"You think on it a minute," Fletch said. He looked toward the house. "While you do, might you grab some food for us?"

Jesse jumped to his feet. "Ma made biscuits for supper. There's a few left. I'll grab what I can. And jam." He hurried into the house his mind awhirl. Was it time for him to leave his family and follow in his brother's footsteps? Find his own destiny amidst the chaos of this war that seemed never to end? Become a man?

By the time he returned with the biscuits and jam, he'd made up his mind. "What do you want me to do?"

"Light out with us in the mornin'."

It was all Jesse had thought about for the past year. Getting even with the men who had beaten him and strung up Pappy. Yankees. And his former neighbors, Bond and Dagley. He wanted them to pay. All of them. Now, it would be sooner rather than later.

This was one conversation Jesse didn't want to have, but he had no choice. He talked to himself as he walked from the barn to the house, trying to decide how best to tell his ma he was leaving in the morning to join up with Frank and Quantrill. He was only sixteen, but lots of boys his age rode with the guerillas. For many of them, it was the only family they had. Sure, he still had a family, but he had debts to collect, and riding with those boys would give him a good start in collecting them.

"Where you been?" his mother asked when he stepped inside.

"In the barn."

"What're you doin' in there? Your chores shoulda been done a long time ago."

"They were, but we got visitors."

Zerelda's eyes widened, and she jumped up from the kitchen table. "What kinda visitors?"

"The kind like Frank."

"Frank? He's here?" She started toward the door.

Jesse blocked her way. "No, Ma, he ain't here. But a couple of the boys he rides with are."

She cocked her head. "What do they want?"

"Me."

She released a startled cry. "You're a boy."

"A boy old enough to bring in a good crop of tobacco all by hisself and keep this place running for the past year. I been using a gun since I was knee-high to a toad, and I been practicing. I was sure old enough to get beat by those militia boys. And I'm old enough to ride with Frank."

"Why didn't he come?"

"Didn't want to come near in case they're watching the place. Or he was recognized. The boys came instead."

Zerelda looked him straight in the eyes. "Do you want to go?"

Jesse didn't hesitate. "Yeah, Ma, I do."

Her shoulders stiffened. She drew in a deep breath. "Then go. We'll manage here." She grabbed Jesse's hand. "Avenge yourself and Pappy and what they done to ya."

*

In the darkness, Jesse, Frank and several other Quantrill men slid along the walls of the barn closest to their prey's house.

Jesse had trouble controlling his excitement. Gooseflesh tore up his arms and his heart beat like he'd run a mile at breakneck speed.

The day had finally come. Retribution was at hand.

Peyton Long, on Jesse's right, leaned toward him and whispered, "He's in the front room. I kin see him movin' around in the light. Won't be long now." Peyton grinned, his teeth flashing in the moonlight.

Jesse forced down his anticipation of what was about to happen. This was the home of Brantley Bond and it was time for him to pay what he owed the James family. He and Frank were about to collect.

Frank nudged Jesse from his other side. "You ready?"

"Been ready for more'n a year."

In silence, the Bushwhackers rushed toward the house.

Crouched below the window to the right of the front door, Jesse waited for the signal, his heart pounding. There was a shrill whistle. He stood and shattered the window with the handle of his pistol.

Inside, Brantley Bond scurried for cover.

Jesse fired several times into the room.

The front door crashed open. Jesse's companions ran inside, their guns roaring.

"Don't! Please don't," Bond begged. But his pleas fell on deaf ears, the same way Jesse's, his mother's and Pappy's had a year ago.

More guns exploded. The smell of spent powder filled the air.

Then there was silence.

Jesse stared through the window at the man sprawled on the floor, covered in blood, who had once been his family's friend.

Bile threatened to come up. He managed to keep it down as he hurried away from the house. He was a man now and had to act like one. Brantley Bond was dead. His stepfather had been partially avenged. One more had to pay.

The next day the party of Bushwhackers headed to the home of Alvis Dagley. Within minutes of their arrival, Dagley, too, was dead.

Debt collected.

*

September 27, 1864

Jesse studied the rolling landscape that led into Centralia, Missouri. He removed his hat, finger-combed the hair off his forehead, then slid it back on. He looked into the bright sky, and pondered the five months that had passed since he became a guerilla.

In June or July of '64, Jesse couldn't remember which, he and Frank had left Quantrill after Quantrill split with some of his men following a disagreement while wintering in Texas. Jesse rode with Bill Anderson, Frank, and George Todd now. Even though there'd been a split, the splintered commands still rode under Quantrill.

A chill ran up Jesse's spine when he thought of what drove "Bloody" Bill Anderson. First, his father had been murdered by a former friend who turned loyalist. Then in August of '63, before Jesse left his family to join the guerillas, three of Bill's sisters were arrested for spying and aiding their brother and the Bushwhackers.

The girls had been confined in a makeshift prison in Kansas City with several other women and, only days after their arrest, the building collapsed. Bill was certain it was intentional.

Fourteen-year-old Josephine Anderson was killed. Her sisters, Mary Ellen, sixteen, and Janie, ten, were both severely injured. Two cousins of the Younger boys had also died, and one more girl several days later. Other kin of men in Quantrill's command had also been injured, firing up more than one guerilla.

Josephine's death sent Bill into a wild rage.

The relations of the maimed and murdered girls got their revenge a week later when they rode with Quantrill into abolitionist Lawrence, Kansas, with over four hundred men. Nearly two hundred men and soldiers, mostly boys, were killed that day. Well over a hundred buildings were left in flames upon their retreat.

Jesse'd felt nothing but joy when he heard the news about Lawrence. He had no use for Yankees, especially not holier-than-thou abolitionists. And especially not Senator James Lane who resided there. He was the coward who, with his Jayhawkers, had ordered most of the atrocities that had occurred along the Kansas/Missouri border over the past years, which included robbery, murder, and the destruction and burning of more than one town.

Jesse recalled Lane's proclamation of '61 to the people of Missouri. He'd outright admitted the excesses committed upon their persons and property. Then he'd given warning for them to lay down their arms and seek protection...or be prepared for the "stern visitations of war upon the rebels *and* their allies." Jesse shivered in the warm September breeze. He understood now, more than ever, that *allies* meant families. Women, children and the old. It didn't matter.

Quantrill and his men had ridden into Lawrence that early August morning in '63 to mete out some "stern visitations" of their own. Like Lane and his Jayhawkers had done in Missouri in Butler, Harrisonville, Papinville, Morristown, and Osceola over the years. They rode into Lawrence chanting "remember Osceola" and "remember the murdered girls." Lane had burned Osceola nearly to the ground. And who could forget the girls killed in the jail collapse in Kansas City on the week before. Not Bill Anderson.

Jesse felt no remorse for those killed in abolitionist Lawrence that day. They'd chosen their side, and they'd died for it. Hell, most of the "men" who'd ridden with Quantrill that day were barely fifteen to twenty years old. Boys themselves who rode with Charley because of atrocities committed against their families by Jayhawkers, Redlegs, and the 7th Kansas Cavalry in their war on Missourians. A war that had started long before the firing on Fort Sumter and formal declaration of war.

After the raid on Lawrence, chased by Union forces, Quantrill, Anderson, and their commands had hightailed it back to Missouri. But when it got too hot, they'd headed for Texas.

Frank and the rest of the Bushwhackers had terrorized North Texas for months before returning to Missouri in the spring of '64, just before Fletch Taylor showed up at the James farm to recruit Jesse.

Jesse sighed. Because of the bad blood between Quantrill and Anderson, some of the guerillas, not including Quantrill, were camped outside the small town of Centralia, a little over twenty miles north of Columbia and halfway between Kansas City and St. Louis. As many as four hundred men rode with them. Every one had an axe to grind with the Yankees, the least of whom were Jesse, Frank, and Bill Anderson himself.

In the year since the building collapse and death of his sister, Bill had come to be known as "Bloody" Bill because of his murderous rampages. More than once, Jesse watched him add knots to a length of rope he carried. With a vicious scowl, Bill snapped the knots into place, each one signifying another man he'd killed.

Jesse was sure glad to be riding *with* Bloody Bill Anderson and not *against* him. Although he shared a similar rage, some of Jesse's had been assuaged with the deaths of Bond and Dagley.

For all the men he'd killed, Bill's had not.

Jesse sat his horse, still pondering the events that had brought him to this place, when Bill shouted, "Boys, it's time to go into Centralia. Make yourselves to home once you git there. Make them Yanks sorry to be a part of the Union they so dearly love." He fisted his hand above his head. "They'll remember who we are and what we done today."

Frank, riding with Jesse today, cheered along with his brother and the others riding into town.

Jesse felt like a bird soaring on the wind as they swooped into Centralia screaming, shooting, and promising death to anyone who opposed them. Most of the residents gave way, allowing easy access to anything the guerillas wanted. Those who didn't were sorry. Many of the boys got drunk. Frank disappeared. Jesse didn't know where.

When a stage rolled in about eleven that morning, it was stopped and surrounded.

Jesse stood beside Peyton Long outside the coach. Peyton pulled the door open and stuck his head inside. "Where you headed?" he asked the passengers.

"We're from Columbia on our way to Mexico, not far from here, for the Democratic Congressional convention there," one man said.

"Is that a fact?" Peyton drawled.

Several of the men offered their names when asked, but it mattered not who they were.

"Hand out your money," Long told them.

"We're Southern men and Confederate sympathizers," several of the passengers challenged.

Long snorted. "What do we care? Hell's full of such Southern men. Why ain't you in the army, or out fighting?"

Jesse hooted with laughter. Peyton moved aside and Jesse stepped into the stage to search the passengers for money and to determine whether they had lied about who they were and why they were here.

Jesse had only just begun when the St. Louis train blew it's whistle down the tracks. He poked his head out the door.

Peyton, standing beside the coach, smiled with malice. "New fodder."

Jesse jumped out, landing like a cat on his feet.

"Let's go see what we got." Peyton slapped Jesse on the shoulder and headed toward the slowing train.

Some of the boys were piling railroad ties from a stack nearby onto the tracks ahead of the train. "Why are they doin' that?" Jesse asked Peyton.

"That's why." Peyton thrust his thumb toward the train. It was speeding up.

Moments later, the guerillas opened fire on the accelerating locomotive. Screams echoed from the forward cars filled with civilian passengers. The train slowed to a stop and the Bushwhackers surrounded it.

Jesse followed Bill and Peyton onto the train. Frank appeared behind them, along with Arch Clement and another guerilla. The six men strode through the cars filled with terrified passengers, then headed for the express car.

"Where're the keys?" Bill asked the express messenger when they got inside. The man hesitated and Bill smashed his pistol across the top of his head.

Blood streamed down the man's face. He put his hands in front of him. "All right, all right." He handed Bill the keys to the safe with shaking hands.

Bill flung open the door. His eyes grew wide when he pulled out a stack of money. He waved it around. "Lookie what I found."

Jesse's heart thumped. "How much you think is there?"

Bill ran it through his fingers. "Near to three thousand Yankee dollars, if'n I had to guess."

Peyton whistled.

Frank nodded and smiled.

Jesse whooped with Arch and the other man.

"There's more to be found on this train. I guarantee it," Bill told them. He stood and headed back through the coaches, yelling, threatening, and taking whatever he could lay his hands on from the frightened travelers.

Jesse jumped and whirled, his gun ready, when several of the boys shot their pistols in the air. With a smirk, he fired too. More than one frightened passenger screamed.

With threats and insults, the guerillas worked their way to the soldiers' coach at the rear.

Long went ahead with Arch Clements and the other man. When they reached the car carrying the soldiers, Arch yelled inside, "Surrender, you are prisoners of war!"

"We will have to surrender, for we are unarmed," came the weak response from inside the car.

Bill, Jesse, and Frank followed Arch and Peyton inside.

Bill studied the frightened soldiers. "Take off them uniforms," he ordered.

They offered no resistance. Jesse, trying to make his bones among the more seasoned men, kicked and threatened them like Bill's other men did.

Anderson waved his gun in the air. "Get off," he ordered when the Federals had stripped to their underwear.

Their hands in the air, the nearly two dozen Union soldiers were marched off the train.

"Line up over there." Bill pointed along the side of the tracks where the humiliated men would be in full view of the civilians from the train and in town.

Arch stepped beside Bill. "What are you going to do with them fellows, Captain?" Jesse heard him ask.

"Parole them, of course." Anderson's look told Jesse he meant something very different.

Arch laughed. "I thought so." He sobered a moment then added, "You might pick out two or three of them to exchange for Cave, if you can."

Jesse knew that Cave Wyatt, a sergeant in Bill's company, was being held by the Federals in Columbia. He'd been taken prisoner after being wounded in a recent skirmish.

Anderson grinned. "Oh, one will be enough for that." He stepped closer to the Federals. "Boys, is there a sergeant among you?"

No one answered.

Bill asked again. "I say, is there a sergeant in this line?"

To Jesse's surprise, a man stepped forward.

Anderson pursed his lips and nodded. He pointed to Hiram Litton and Richard Ellington. "Take him to someplace safe and protect him."

Jesse never ceased to be amazed at how quickly, and without question, Anderson's men did as they were told. The sergeant was whisked away by Litton and Ellington.

That sergeant had no idea how lucky he was, Jesse mused. Bill would keep him safe in order to trade for Cave, for that reason and that reason alone. Jesse considered, if he had to choose between being the sergeant or any of these other Federals, he'd choose the sergeant. He would live to be traded. The others...

Bill turned back to Arch. "Arch, you take charge of the firing party and, when I give the word, pour hell into them."

Jesse'd been right. These soldiers were going to die. He studied the guerillas around him, glad to be on this side of the two and three revolvers each one carried.

Anderson closed his eyes and snapped his head up then down.

"Fire!" Arch Clements yelled.

Guns exploded. At least a dozen Federals fell on the first volley. Others broke and ran. Some begged for mercy, but were given none. One man, large in stature, charged the guerillas. He knocked five of them to the ground and was shot five times for his effort. He clawed his way under the depot's platform, but was dragged out and shot in the head.

One by one, any soldier who wasn't already dead, was killed.

When Jesse looked around, the guerillas were doing unspeakable things to the bodies. Memories of being beaten and Pappy being hanged flashed through his mind. The anger he'd experienced every day since then bubbled in his belly until it boiled like liquid in a pot over a high flame.

These men were Yankees and Yankees deserved everything they got. Jesse slipped his sword from its sheath and swung his first blow. Then another and another.

The killing rage was upon him, as it was with the other guerillas. They didn't stop until every dead soldier had been scalped and mutilated in the most horrific ways.

Blood covered Jesse's body, hands, and face. He started to shake. He should be ashamed for the evil they'd done today and his part in it. But he recalled again *why* he was here, riding with Bloody Bill Anderson. His shoulders squared and the shaking stopped. A quiet calm fell over him and his lip lifted in a slight grin. Revenge was sweet.

Bill pointed at the train and shouted, "Fire her up."

Once emptied of civilian passengers, the guerillas filled the cars with wood and set the train ablaze. They sent it rolling westward to jump the tracks and crash. Or burn to its frame when it finally stopped.

With the train blazing its way out of town, Bill ordered his men to mount up. They raced toward the bushwhacker encampment, Jesse yelling as loudly as any of them.

Anderson's command rejoined the rest of the guerillas camped southeast of town. Dave Pool and several others were sent out to reconnoiter whether they were being followed.

On their return, they reported a troop of Federals had just ridden into town.

Such a malicious grin curled Bill's lips that, for the second time that day, Jesse was glad to be riding *with* Anderson and not *against* him.

77

"Here's where we'll really make our mark," Anderson told his men. "We'll set a trap for them blue bellies and show 'em once-and-for-all that we're a force to be reckoned with!"

The commanders came up with a plan. Jesse was proud to be included in the small detachment that was dispatched to lure the troops into their trap.

Jesse, Frank, Peyton, Dave and John Pool, and five others, mounted and headed toward town. They rode close enough to be seen by the Federals, then raced back to camp, the soldiers in hot pursuit.

The Federals followed them right into an open field outside of town—straight into the guerilla trap.

"You done good," Anderson told Jesse when he rejoined the rest of the company waiting for the unsuspecting soldiers racing toward them.

Jesse felt emboldened by his commander's praise. At the front of the line set to lead the charge, Anderson's men couldn't contain their surprise when the Federals reined to a halt and dismounted.

Laughter filtered through the Bushwhacker ranks.

"Are they crazy?" Clements asked aloud. "They're gonna meet us afoot?"

Jesse was dumbfounded. To meet the guerillas on foot was suicide. He watched in disbelief as every fifth soldier took hold of the horses left by the dismounted men.

His attention was captured when Bill shouted, "Boys, when we charge, break through the line and keep straight on for their horses. Keep straight on for their horses," he repeated.

Anderson's line held steady.

Jesse's heart raced. The morning and early afternoon of looting and terrorism had gone quickly for Jesse. Now, as the hands of the clock reached toward four in the afternoon, time seemed to stand still. Anxious and charged with excitement for what was about to happen, he waited.

Unaware of what they faced, outnumbered at least two to one, and afoot against some of the best horsemen and marksmen alive, the Federal commander shouted at the only Bushwhackers visible in the tall weeds and prairie grasses. Anderson's men.

"We are ready. Come on!" When the bushwhackers didn't ride out to meet them, he taunted. "Wait for us you damned cowards!"

Anderson's men did wait. Until Bill lifted his hat and whirled it around his head. The order to charge. The line surged ahead.

Jesse raced forward, leveling his gun at any Federal in his sights. Man after man went down. He rode straight for the commander. Fired. The man fell.

The pasture exploded as the remaining guerillas hidden on the fringes of the field joined the fight.

It was over in three minutes.

Jesse linked up with the guerillas who chased the "horse handlers" as they raced from the field. One by one they were found and cut down. It didn't matter how far they ran.

When he rejoined the company later that day, Jesse got the count of Federal dead from Dave Poole. Dave claimed there were a hundred and thirty killed. Most with one shot to the head.

*

Late July/August, 1865

Jesse shifted in the soft bed. He was convalescing at his aunt and uncle's home near Kansas City from a gunshot wound to his chest. It chafed him every time he thought about being shot while carrying a white flag trying to surrender!

He still hurt, but every day the pain lessened. Boredom was taking hold, and that was almost as bad.

There was an ache in his gut, too, that had nothing to do with his wound. It had to do with the fact that so many of his comrades were dead. Including "Bloody" Bill, killed not far from where he called home. It happened near Albany, Missouri, in October of '64, only a month after Centralia.

Jesse stifled a groan. After Bill's death, he and Frank rode with Archie Clements and his boys, even though they'd all known the war couldn't go on much longer. The Confederacy was beaten. In more ways than one. Every man lost in the ranks was one fewer to fight. There were none to replace them, while the Union seemed to have an unending supply of fodder to refill their ranks.

Most of the men in gray wore raggedy uniforms and shoes, if they had a uniform or shoes at all. And food was always a question. It was hard to fight a war when you were hungry.

They'd all known it was only a matter of time until the South threw up her hands and said "enough."

That time came on April 9, 1865, at a place called Appomattox Courthouse in Virginia. The beloved state General Robert E. Lee called home. *Had* called home once upon a time.

Jesse recalled hearing about the assassination of Abraham Lincoln less than a week after the surrender. A slight grin curled the corner of his mouth when he remembered rejoicing with Archie and his men like it was the Fourth of July.

But the surrender didn't stop Jesse from riding with Archie and his guerillas in the name of the Confederacy. Until Jesse was shot a month later in a skirmish with Union troops outside Lexington, Missouri. Where he'd tried to surrender.

He was taken to his mother and Pappy in Rulo, Nebraska, where they'd fled following the issuance of Order Number 9 in January of '65 while the war was still on. That Order had, in essence, exiled them and other "undesirables" from their homes in Clay County. Undesirables like Lou McCoy, the woman whose arrest had incited the Missouri City raid in May of '63 that had led to Jesse's beating and Pappy's neck stretching.

While in Nebraska, Jesse learned his former commander, Charley Quantrill, had been wounded, arrested, and died in prison in Kentucky in early June. It had been a difficult blow for him to take. He'd truly believed Charley was indestructible.

The end was coming quick and hard for the men who had fought on the fringes of the Confederacy.

Now that the war was officially over, Jesse was back in Missouri to finish recuperating. Settled at his aunt and uncle's home near Kansas City, he'd found a new reason to live.

Although his kin were attentive in his care, it was Zee that made the difference in his healing. There was nothing in his drab life right now except thoughts of his petite cousin Zee, named for his own mother, Zerelda. When Zee entered the room, Jesse thought of nothing but making her smile. He wanted to get better. For her.

"And how are you this beautiful morning?" Zee's question when she swept into the room interrupted Jesse's woolgathering. Her smile brightened his bedchamber even before she flung the curtains wide to let in the sunshine.

Startled by her sudden appearance, Jesse took a moment then said, "I reckon I'll live. Thanks to you."

She blushed, and Jesse's heart swelled. Her innocence made him wonder what might have become of him if the war hadn't happened. If he hadn't been beaten and the world turned upside down. Might he have become a preacher like his father and uncle? Or a gentleman tobacco farmer? He'd done a pretty good job raising that crop before he'd joined up with Charley and become a marauding guerilla. A man other men feared.

So much time had been lost. Time that might have been spent becoming a different man. One who might have gotten to know Zee sooner.

Jesse chuckled at Zee's flaming cheeks. Despite all he'd suffered, he was happy here.

Because of her.

He smiled. He would get better and Zee would become his wife. Of that he had no doubt.

The war was over, the rest of his life was a blank page.

One he had yet to write.

The Rest of the Story

History is not an exact science. That has been proven true to me again and again during my research for this story. We do the best we can to glean the facts from the data we have. These are the facts as I have found them.

Some accountings say the James family raised hemp on their 100-acre farm. Others say tobacco. Perhaps it was both.

It's uncertain whether the day of Jesse's beating occurred on May 23 or May 25, as the dates differ in different accounts.

Jesse was whipped with a rope and/or a saber when beaten at his farm. This entailed using a rope like a whip or the flat side/edge of a sword and slapping it against his body.

After Reuben Samuel's neck was "stretched" and his subsequent arrest, he took the Oath of Allegiance and was paroled from prison in St. Joseph two weeks later on June 4, 1863. Zerelda was also paroled from prison in St. Joseph, taking the Oath of Allegiance on June 5, 1863.

It's not proven that Jesse killed Brantley Bond and/or Alvin Dagley, but he was (allegedly) at both events.

In August of '64, it is reported Jesse was shot (the first time) in the chest. It's uncertain whether it was stealing a saddle from a farmer or in an engagement with Federals.

Weeks later, on September 27th, Jesse was with Bill Anderson at Centralia. It has been reported that Jesse killed Major Johnston there. According to Frank James in an article printed in *You All Look Brave Enough to Hang a Woman (see references),* quoted from the *Magazine* section of the *Saint Louis Republic* dated August 5th, 1900, Frank said it was "likely" Jesse killed the major.

Major A.V.E. Johnston was in command of troops in nearby Paris, Missouri. On September 26th (the day prior to the massacre) he learned of guerilla movements near Centralia and headed there to take up the chase. He'd been ordered by General C. B. Fisk, Commanding, to "exterminate the murderous thieving Bushwhackers," in this part of Missouri. (This would explain Frank's statement below in the *Magazine* article in 1900 about Johnston coming out to "hunt" them.)

Some reports state twenty-one soldiers were taken off the train at Centralia, others say twenty-three and others twenty-four. Some show Frank as being among the men in Centralia at the time of the massacre, others say he was not. After Centralia, a Union militia captain wrote a report stating he was certain **both** James boys had taken part in the massacre in town and ambush of Federal soldiers afterward. Frank says he was with the other guerillas who remained behind when Anderson's command of eighty men (or was it only thirty, as Frank states in the *Magazine* article?) went into town, but that he was there when the soldiers who chased them (Johnston and his troops) were surprised and killed.

The following is a quote from Frank James in the *Magazine* article about Centralia:

"When great, big, grown men, with full possession of all their faculties, refer to that battle as 'The Centralia Massacre,' I think they are pleading the baby act. We did not seek the fight. Johnston **foolishly came out to hunt us, and he found us**. Then we killed him and his men. Wouldn't he have killed every one of us if he had had a chance? What is war for if it isn't to kill people for a principle? The Yankee soldiers tried to kill every one of the Southern soldiers, and the soldiers from the South tried to kill all the Yanks, and that's all there is of it." (Note, this was the same tactic Crazy Horse used on December 21, 1866. Approximately 2,000 Lakota warriors hid north of Fort Phil Kearney when an attack was made on a party of woodcutters from the fort. Colonel Fetterman was ordered to go to their aid. Crazy Horse and ten decoy warriors then rode into view of the fort to lure the soldiers out. When an artillery round was fired at the decoys, they fled. Colonel Fetterman and his eighty men chased after Crazy Horse and his decoys, as planned. The soldiers rode right into a trap and were massacred. No man survived.) (From: https://www.history.com/this-day-in-history/indians-massacre-fetterman-and-eighty-soldiers#)

Frank also stated in his accounting that only one citizen of Centralia was killed and that it was in a "drunken row." However, other reports say several civilians were killed when they didn't give in to the guerillas. (*History of Centralia, Missouri*: By Edgar T. Rodemyre, Published 1936 by the Centralia Historical Society-see references)

The horses Major Johnston commandeered to chase the guerillas were farm/plow horses, unused to gunfire. Seeing *only* Anderson's men, unaware the remainder of the guerillas were hidden on the fringes of the field, the major gave the order for his soldiers to dismount and for every fifth man to take charge of the skittish animals. In this way, the *infantry* soldiers could reload their long-range muskets more easily and the skittish horses were taken out of the battle equation. After the first line of soldiers were cut down, the "fifth men" were tracked down and killed. (*History*)

Thomas Goodman, the Federal soldier that stepped out of line when asked if any man among the captured men was a sergeant, was taken to a stable and kept under guard on a farm where the Bushwhackers had set up camp. (Most likely to be used as an exchange for the imprisoned bushwhacker sergeant Cave Wyatt.) Goodman escaped about ten days later. In 1864 he wrote an accounting of the battle and had it published. (*History*)

Regarding the Raid on Lawrence on August 21, 1863, conflicting evidence has surfaced as to whether the town was as undefended as stated in reports following the incident, and that the killing by Quantrill's men was **not** as "indiscriminate" as reported. It is argued that women and children were not harmed but were, in fact, protected by the invaders. It is suggested in a book by James C. Edwards, *What Really Happened? Quantrill's Raid on Lawrence, Kansas, Revisiting the Evidence*, Shotwell Publishing, Columbia, South Carolina, 2021, that as many as 550 soldiers (and arms at the armory) were in town, prepared for a Confederate raid, and as many as 50 "Redlegs" were there, as well, when Quantrill and his men rode in early that morning while everyone slept. It is also suggested there was a killing "list" of those men the raiders hunted. Men who had committed acts of violence against Missourians, such as Senator James Lane (who hid in a corn field to save his life that day).

There are numerous other "discrepancies" between "original" findings and other first-hand accounts by survivors that show the raiders not to be the monsters they've been depicted to be throughout the years. History is written by the victors, so you decide. It's long in the past and it will never be known what the *full* truth is.

Remember Cole Younger? Why did he fight for the Confederacy, as a guerilla with Quantrill and as a regular soldier, when his father was a Unionist?

At a party when Cole was only seventeen, he was accused by Federal Lieutenant Irvin Walley of being a spy. Walley threatened to hang him and hounded Cole and his family following his declaration. He even harassed Cole's mother and sisters when they fled Cass County to Waverly, Missouri. When Cole's father, the former Mayor of Harrisonville, was murdered on his return from a business trip to Kansas City, was Walley the man who did the deed in his frustration at not being able to catch Cole? If Henry Younger was killed in a robbery (and not for revenge), why was the nearly $3,000 he carried still on him when he was found?

After Cole joined Quantrill, the Federals learned his mother was feeding the bushwhackers and forced her to burn down her own house.

In Bullitt County, Kentucky, Henry McGruder was another young man who became a guerilla by circumstances. When McGruder, while plowing the field of his widowed mother, objected to a troop of Union men taking his horse, he was stripped and beaten near to death. He vowed revenge on his aggressors and was good to his word. With another horse, three pistols, and a double-barrel shotgun, he rode into the midst of the sixteen men who had beaten him. They were stealing more horses at the time. Henry killed ten of them. The final six he chased for miles until he caught and killed them too. After that he was never known to take a prisoner. He killed anyone who fell into his hands. He was only sixteen at the time he was beaten and his mother disrespected. (It's uncertain *how* she was disrespected.)

"Bloody" Bill Anderson was killed on October 26, 1864, by Union soldiers near Albany, Missouri, present-day Orrick. His rope with 54 knots, each representing a kill, was found on his person.

From *You All Look Brave Enough to Hang a Woman*: "On December 4th, 1864 Quantrill announced he was going to Kentucky and some 30 to 40 men went with him. Frank went with him on his last ride. On June [May] 11th, 1865, Quantrill's band was surprised by a Federal force in Nelson County, Kentucky. During the fight Quantrill was wounded in the back, paralyzed and captured. Many of his men were killed. By a stroke of fortune, Frank was not there that day but was with a second group of guerillas a few miles away. Quantrill died a captive on June 6th, 1865. The remaining guerillas surrendered on July 25th, 1865 at Samuels Depot, Nelson County, Kentucky."

Lest we forget the "Drake" Constitution, (Officially known as the Missouri Constitution of 1865, adopted by the Missouri state legislature on April 8, 1865, which included a requirement that all Missourians who wished to vote, hold public office, teach, or be the trustee of a corporation must take an oath of loyalty, swearing that they **had never supported the Southern cause in any way or had even spoken in favor of it**): (http://www.civilwarmo.org/educators/resources/info-sheets/constitution-1865-drake-constitution)

- The new Constitution banned the practice of slavery without exception.
- It restricted the rights of former rebels and rebel sympathizers. (Above)
- Part of the constitution was embodied in what became known as the "Ironclad" or "Kucklebur" Oath, which was contained in Article 2. It required teachers, lawyers, clergy, and all voters to promise that they had not committed a *long list of disloyal*

acts. These groups were targeted for their influence over the general population.

- In addition, with support of the rural delegates, Drake forced the evacuation of the offices of all judges, lawyers, and sheriffs and restricted the right to vote to only those who had been loyal to Missouri and the Union. This ensured the election of Radicals to all the newly vacated positions.

Disenfranchised by the Drake Constitution, those who had fought for the Confederacy, as regular soldiers or as guerillas like the James brothers, were unable to support themselves. They also lived in constant fear of reprisals against them and their families.

Most guerillas went home and tried to live peacefully. Jesse and Frank did settle down on their family farmstead for three or four years. Jesse even joined a church and was baptized. But his and Frank's past, the inability to be welcomed back into society, and the encroachment of the railroad purchasing the land of former known Confederates for **pennies on the dollar**, kept them at the mercy of the men they hated most. Yankees. Angry and without other recourse, they eventually turned to robbery. (*Jesse James - The Last Rebel of the Civil War?* see references)

On February 13, 1866, Frank, and most likely Cole Younger, participated in the robbery of the Clay County Savings Bank in Liberty, Missouri. There, a nineteen-year-old bystander (some reports say he was seventeen) was killed. It's uncertain if Jesse was there, possibly still recuperating from the wound to his lung he suffered when trying to surrender to Union forces at Lexington in May of 1865. However, we must remember he rode with Anderson at Centralia only a month after his first chest wound. Will we ever know for sure if he was there or not?

Jesse and Frank were relatively unheard of until December 7, 1869, when they walked into the Daviess County Savings Association in Gallatin, Missouri, and allegedly robbed it. Jesse mistook the bank president, Mr. John W. Sheets, for Samuel P. Cox, the commander of the Union forces that had killed Bloody Bill Anderson. In his mistaken rage, Jesse murdered Sheets and killed another man. (It is currently being questioned whether Jesse and Frank were at Gallatin.)

While trying to escape, Jesse was thrown off his horse and dragged thirty or forty feet before freeing himself. Frank returned for his brother and the two escaped, but Jesse's mare, Kate, was left behind. The horse was recognized to be Jesse's and the residents of Gallatin put up a $1,500 reward for the arrest of the James brothers. Thus began their careers as wanted men. (*Jesse James and the Road to Gallatin* – see references)

Jesse eventually married Zee Mimms, but not until nine years later on April 24, 1874, when the James/Younger Gang was in full outlaw mode.

On January 26, 1875, the James farm was attacked once again. This time, (purportedly) by the Pinkertons. Zerelda James lost her arm and Jesse's nine-year-old half-brother, Archie (named for Archie Clements), died following the explosion of an incendiary device thrown into their kitchen. The Pinkertons had gone to the farm looking for Jesse and Frank who were supposed to be there at the time. They were not.

For years the James and Younger boys robbed banks, trains, and even stagecoaches. In September of 1876, members of the James/Younger Gang attempted to rob the bank in Northfield, Minnesota. When the cashier refused to open the vault, he was killed, allegedly by Jesse.

Aware of the strangers in town, the residents were ready when the first alarm sounded. A giant manhunt followed. Two of the gang members were killed. Cole, Jim and a severely injured Bob Younger, were captured. Jesse and Frank escaped.

Having eluded the law Jesse James, now calling himself Thomas Howard, lived quietly with Zee and his two children in St. Joseph for several years. But that type of living wasn't for him. A new gang was organized, including the brothers Robert and Charley Ford. On April 3, 1882, Jesse was shot in the head by Bob Ford (who had made a deal with Governor Crittendon) when Jesse set aside his guns and stepped up on a chair to straighten a picture on the wall. Jesse died, leaving his family penniless. (It is argued the man who was killed was not Jesse but a distrusted family member with similar DNA. That, however, is another story...)

Jesse was 5'8", 155 pounds, and vain about his appearance. He was a Democrat, left-handed, and had a high voice. He knew the books of the Bible and could recite passages from it. He also knew and sang religious hymns. He was the type of man people turned to look at when he entered a room.

At some point in his life, Jesse got the nickname "Dingus." He didn't like to cuss, so when he blew the tip of his finger off, he reportedly said, "that's the dod-dingus pistol I ever saw."

Frank's nickname was "Buck."

Frank James, after giving up his life of crime, was acquitted of all the deeds he was accused of committing and became an upstanding citizen. He died at the age of 72 from prostate cancer. However, once Frank passed, several stories surfaced placing him at those same robberies he'd been acquitted of committing. One such story (from *You All Look Brave Enough to Hang a Woman*) reads:

"Frank died, but not the legends. His death propagated them. When Frank died in 1915 Mr. Horace Sublette of Missouri City corroborated one. He went to the editor of the Liberty Tribune, Irving Gilmer…with the story that Frank made him [Horace] row Frank across the river, swimming his horse behind, on the night of the Liberty Bank robbery. He [Frank] told Horace that he would kill him if he told anyone he was there that day. Horace felt safe to tell the story now that Frank was dead."

Was Frank the brains of the gang and Jesse the muscle? Had something shifted so greatly in Jesse after his beating he never returned to "normal?" Then did his being hounded and hunted after the war for having ridden with the south push him into his lawless life?

The following passage was written in an obituary for Jesse by John Newman Edwards, editor of the *Sedalia Democrat* (and ally to Jesse throughout his outlaw career):

"We called him outlaw, and he was – but fate made him so. When the war closed Jesse James had no home…hunted, shot, driven away…a price upon his head – what else could the man do…except what he did?…When he was hunted he turned savagely about and hunted his hunters."

You, the reader, must decide what made Jesse James, and so many others, the men they became.

Resources/Suggested Reading

History of Centralia, Missouri: By Edgar T. Rodemyre, Published 1936 by the Centralia Historical Society

You All Look Brave Enough to Hang a Woman by Jay Jackson and John Moloski, Published by the Burnt District Press, Harrisonville, MO, 2015

Lou's Story: She Adder or Patriot? by D.L. Rogers, KDP/Amazon, 2019
https://www.amazon.com/D.-L.-Rogers/e/B00L2FDNBU

What Really Happened? Quantrill's Raid on Lawrence, Kansas: Revisiting the Evidence, James C. Edwards, Shotwell Publishing, LLC, Columbia, SC, 2021

Internet sites used:

7 Things You May Not Know About Jesse James: https://www.history.com/news/7-things-you-might-not-know-about-jesse-james

Jesse James Biography – Facts, Childhood, Family Life & Achievements:
https://www.thefamouspeople.com/profiles/jesse-james-3887.php

Biography: Jesses James / American Experience / Official Site / PBS:

https://www.pbs.org/wgbh/americanexperience/features/james-jesse/#:-text

Historic Missourians: Jesse James:
https://historicmissourians.shsmo.org/jesse-james#:~:text=Early%20Years

American Outlaw: 10 Facts About Jesse James:
https://www.historyhit.com/facts-about-jesse-james/

Geneology Trails: The James Family:
HTTP://GENEALOGYTRAILS.COM/KEN/JESSE_JAMES.HTML

Jesse James – Wikipedia:
https://en.wikipedia.org/wiki/Jesse_James

Jesse James:
http://www.fresnostate.edu/folklore/ballads/FR379.html

History: This Day, October 26, in History:
https://www.history.com/this-day-in-history/bloody-bill-anderson-killed

Civil War on the Western Border:
https://civilwaronthewesternborder.org/encyclopedia/anderson-william-%E2%80%9Cbloody-bill%E2%80%9D

American Experience: Jesse James/Guerilla Tactics:
https://www.pbs.org/wgbh/americanexperience/features/james-guerrilla/

How Jesse James Went from Confederate Guerilla to American Folk Hero:
https://allthatsinteresting.com/jesse-james

Jesse James and the Road to Gallatin:
https://truewestmagazine.com/article/jesse-james-and-the-road-to-gallatin/

Jesse James – The Last Rebel of the Civil War? – The Cleveland Civil War Roundtable:
https://www.clevelandcivilwarroundtable.com/jesse-james-the-last-rebel-of-the-civil-war/

"Bloody" Bill Anderson – Wikipedia:
https://en.wikipedia.org/wiki/William_T._Anderson

"Bloody Bill" Anderson killed – HISTORY:
www.history.com/this-day-in-history/bloody-bill-anderson-killed

Guerilla Tactics / American Experience / Official Site / PBS:
www.pbs.org/wgbh/americanexperience/features/james-guerilla/

The Third Time's The Charm

1863

"Hurry, Frank! You're going to make us late for church," John Wornall shouted up the stairs to his eight-year-old son. "Your mother is already in the carriage, waiting for you to get down he—"

Frank barreled down the staircase, past his father and out the open foyer door, pulling his jacket on as he ran. "Sorry, Papa. I was...well, I'm ready now," he called over his shoulder before disappearing down the front steps.

"That boy." John chuckled and shook his head. "Mittie!"

The servant girl hurried into the entry hall and curtsied. "Yes, Mr. Wornall."

"We'll be leaving for church now."

"Yes, Sir." She curtsied again.

He studied the teenaged girl he'd taken in when her parents were killed back in '62. Although much older than Frank, the two had become friends. He had to remind his son often that she was a servant and not a guest in their home. Especially not after he gotten arrested because she'd dared Frank to yell "Hurrah for Jeff Davis" at a troop of passing Federals.

Secretly, however, John was happy for the company she gave his son, since he had no siblings.

As long as she didn't cause trouble.

He chuckled and slid on his hat. Frank followed the girl around like a puppy. Because of Frank's tender feelings, John allowed certain class standards to be overlooked to make his son happy during these trying times and no other children in the household except those of their slaves.

John shook his head when he realized he was standing in the very same spot he was a year ago when he was arrested after Mittie's dare.

He'd been taken away, accused of being a southern sympathizer, and threatened with a hanging. The thought of what *might* have happened made him shiver.

He thanked the good Lord every day since then that he'd been able to convince the commander it was nothing more than a childish prank by a boy trying to impress the older girl. John was released that same night, but had nightmares for weeks afterward.

"John! Are you coming?" Eliza called from the carriage out front.

"Yes, yes, I'm coming." He stepped outside and closed the door behind him. His Bible tucked under his arm, he hurried down the steps, set the book on the front seat, and climbed onto the carriage. He enjoyed driving his family to church. Westport was only three miles away and he felt comfortable making the drive himself. Despite the threat of being waylaid by Confederate Rebels or Bushwhackers, or even Kansas Jayhawkers or Redlegs in this prolonged war, he refused to give up spending his Sunday mornings in church.

John picked up the reins and slapped the horse's rump. "Git up!" The bay mare surged forward.

John gave the horse her head. She knew the way to church as well as he did. Of course, there was only one way to go and that was the road they were on.

He lost himself in thoughts about the war. It had been two long years since the start of the rebellion. Prior to that, he'd been one of the most successful men in Jackson County, farming five hundred acres bursting with oats, corn, wheat, and hay. Along with the crops, he raised livestock, horses, cows, pigs, and mules that he sold in Westport.

He frowned and shook his head. Then came the war and he was expected to choose a side. He was a southern man but couldn't make that choice. He had too much to lose. So he played both sides to his advantage. But that didn't always work.

He recalled the day when Colonel Charles "Doc" Jennison, leader of the 7th Kansas Cavalry and known for his brutality toward southerners, had taken over John's home to use as his headquarters. For eight days, Jennison's men burned fences, killed livestock, and destroyed John's crops to provision his men.

During those eight days John and his family had donned their best hospitality and treated Jennison and his men like welcomed guests. That hospitality saved them.

Before Jennison's departure, the colonel confided that he'd gone to John's home to kill him for his southern sympathies. But thanks to John's treatment of him and his men, Jennison changed his mind. In the end, the colonel gave him almost three thousand dollars for damages to his home and left peacefully. To this day, John still couldn't believe his good fortune.

John heard his name being called. He twisted in the seat and spotted his top hand, Hans, waving at him from the field on his left. John waved back. No longer lost in his thoughts, he snapped the reins and the mare surged forward.

They hadn't gone far when horses racing up from behind the carriage caught John's attention. He pulled the mare to the side of the road to let the riders pass.

The troop of Federal soldiers surrounded them instead.

John tipped his hat. "Good morning, friends."

The Union soldier in sergeant's stripes kneed his mount toward the carriage. "Good morning, Sir. I apologize for the delay, but we need a word."

"Must we do this now?" Eliza asked from the rear seat. "We're already late for church."

The sergeant faced Eliza. "This cannot wait, Madam." He turned back to John. "I'm afraid you won't make it to church this morning. Please follow me." He lifted his arm in the direction of the house.

Why did these soldiers want to go to his home? John's palms began to sweat and a chill tore up his spine when he again recalled his other altercations with Federal soldiers.

"What is this about, Sir?"

The sergeant shook his head. "We'll discuss it once we get back."

John had learned not to question the authority of either army. He backed up the horse enough for her to turn around and they started home.

Eliza laid her hand on his shoulder from the back seat. "What's happening?" Fear was obvious in her voice.

"I don't know, but we must do as they say."

"I'm afraid, Papa," Frank whimpered from the rear seat.

John turned around to address his son. "We'll be fine. Don't you worry now."

Eliza cradled Frank under her arm and John turned back to the road.

When they reached the house, John led the way inside. Once Eliza had taken Frank upstairs, John confronted the soldiers. "What is going on? What do you want of me?"

His question was ignored. Several men broke away and began to search the house, and none too carefully. Vases were broken. Precious photos were tossed aside.

"Sir, I protest. There is no need for your men's callousness with my family's belongings. If you tell me what you're looking for, I shall assist you."

"Very well, Mr. Wornall. We are looking for the money you have here."

Taken aback, John frowned. "There is no money here. It's in the bank in town." His mind whirled. *Why do these Federals want my money? Why would they stoop to thievery to get it? If the Union needed money, all they had to do was ask.*

"There's no money hidden in this house?"

"No, Sir. I don't keep any in my home. It would be too easy to be…stolen." He paused a moment, trying to decide how to proceed without making these men angry. He knew soldiers from both sides took what they needed to furnish food and supplies for their men. They called it foraging. He called it thievery. "I shall take you into town, to the bank, and get you whatever you require," he offered.

The sergeant took a step backward. He scrubbed at his bearded chin and shook his head. "No. No. We don't want to do that."

It was then John understood with absolute certainty that these men were not Federals, but Bushwhackers in Federal uniforms. Stolen from where, he didn't want to think about.

The rest of the men fanned out throughout the house. They brought Eliza and Frank, Mittie, and several slaves into the front room.

"Sit and keep your mouths shut," they were told.

Eliza began to speak, but John lifted his hand and shook his head. She snapped her mouth shut, then pulled Frank in close, her eyes wide.

One by one the men returned with small items of value. One man lifted a handful of jewelry. "This is all I found."

Another asked, "What now?" His tone was laced with frustration.

Another stepped forward and, with a smirk, said, "Let's hang him."

Eliza jumped to her feet. "You cannot!" she cried out. "Why would you do such a vile thing? We've done nothing but what you asked."

One of the intruders stepped to Eliza and shoved her into the chair. "Quiet woman. Or we'll hang you too."

Eliza swallowed hard. She fell silent, but the rage on her face reminded John of a mother bear ready to do anything to protect her offspring. Frank squeezed as close as he could to his mama. He buried his face in her chest when she wrapped her arms around him.

John prayed his wife would keep her tongue, no matter what happened.

The leader rubbed his chin with his fingers, pondering the possibility put in front of him.

"Please don't hurt my family," John said, finally able to speak. What could he do? He was outnumbered ten to one and his family would suffer if he did anything to anger these men.

The sergeant grabbed John's hands and tied them behind his back.

"Please. Please don't do this," Eliza begged from her seat.

Frank jumped up and threw his arms around his father's waist. "Papa! Papa!" he screamed.

One of the men grabbed the boy around his belly and tore him from his father, Frank screaming and kicking as he was hurled into his mother's lap. "Don't let him go again," the man ordered her.

Eliza held tight to her son, smoothing his hair and talking softly in his ear, while her eyes shot daggers at the men. Had he been older, John feared the boy would have done something that would have gotten them all killed. Frank eventually calmed down, sniveling in his mother's embrace.

Huddled together across the room, Mittie and the other servants cried softly.

When John's hands were secured behind his back, the leader took him upstairs to the second-floor balcony. His heart raced. He closed his eyes and prayed to God to be spared, and for his family not to be harmed.

Standing on the balcony, John was glad his wife and child couldn't see what was about to happen.

"Where's that rope?" the leader asked from beside John.

One of the men lifted it in his hands. "It's right here."

"You got any last words?" the leader asked John as he tied one end of the rope around the porch rail.

"Please don't hurt my family."

"We're not monsters. We don't make war on women and children. But we do on turncoats who play both sides."

John lifted his chin. "I don't understand. I'm a southern man. You're southern men. Why do you want to kill me?"

"Because you make money from both sides in this war. That ain't my kind of southern man." He put the noose over John's head.

John closed his eyes again and prayed for forgiveness for all his sins. He'd been a good man in most ways. A good father and husband. He held slaves, but treated them well. Yes, he'd played both ends against the middle in this war, but what else could he have done when both sides wanted what he had?

"I'm a business man, doing what I had to do to survive this war," he implored. Perhaps it might sway this man from hanging him.

The man got in his face. "I don't care. It's time to meet your Maker."

"Please tell my family I'm sorry and that I love them." He wanted his last words to be ones of love.

Two men lifted his legs, about to throw him over the rail, when shots erupted.

Bullets whizzed past John's head and slammed into the house, spraying pieces of shattered bricks across the porch. The men dropped his legs, and he landed hard on the balcony floor. The three imposters crawled from the porch into the house using their elbows to propel themselves forward. Their legs dragged behind them like the worms they were.

"We been found out, boys!" the leader shouted as he disappeared through the door. Moments later John heard them pounding down the stairs and out the back door to where their horses were tied.

Between the rails, John spotted a troop of what he presumed to be real Federal soldiers on the road out front. They were shooting at the Bushwhackers as they fled the house in all directions. He had no idea how they'd come to be here, but he thanked God for answering his prayers. He just prayed that his family was out of the way of danger as bullets flew below.

He was able to crawl inside the house. Once he managed to sit up against the wall, he worked at the twine that kept him bound.

Dispatching the Bushwhackers took less than ten minutes, about the same amount of time it took for John to free himself. Able to use his hands, he loosened the noose, pulled it over his head, and hurled it away like a poisonous snake.

Eliza raced up the stairs screaming his name.

"I'm here, Eliza. I'm fine."

When she spotted him on the floor against the wall, she ran to him, dropped to her knees, and cradled him in her arms. Frank, right behind his mother, hurled himself at his father and sobbed. John enfolded both of them in a tight hug.

Mittie stood at the top of the stairs, crushing her apron in her hands. Over and over again she said, "Thank you Lord. Thank you for sparing him. And us."

When the raiders were long gone and John was seated in the front room, the Lieutenant of the Federal troops stomped inside.

John jumped to his feet and put out his hand. "I don't know how to thank you, Sir. You saved my life."

"I was doing my job, Mr. Wornall. But you should thank your man, not me." He waved his white-gloved hand.

Hans, rolling his hat between his fingers, stepped beside the lieutenant.

"You? How?" John asked in disbelief. Then he recalled seeing Hans in the field. "How did you know they weren't real Federals?"

Hans shook his head. "I had dis feeling," he said, his German accent heavier than normal. "When dey made you turn around, I know someting wasn't right. I grab a horse and ride to de Mission."

"He sounded the alarm and here we are," the lieutenant said.

"And not a minute too soon," John added with a grimace.

"I cannot disagree." The lieutenant grinned and nodded.

John sucked in a deep breath. This was the third time he'd faced death since this war began. He prayed to God it was the last.

Afterword

This story is from an accounting I read at the Wornall House when visiting there in early 2022. At the end of the accounting, there is an addition of what Frank wrote in his memoirs regarding the incident once the "real" Federals showed up:

"The band quickly took to their horses, leaving dad to disentangle himself from the noose of rope around his neck. A few minutes later in the soldiers' appearance might have made a great difference in our lives."

References

The Wornall House, 6115 Wornall Road, Kansas City, Missouri 816-444-1858.

The Wornalls & the Civil War – Wornall/Majors
https://www.wornallmajors.org/explore/wornallcivilwar/

Johnny Clem – Drummer Boy of Chickamauga

Newark, Ohio, May 1861

Ten-year-old John "Johnny" Clem was almost home from what *should* have been his day at school. Instead, he'd done what he did on many a school day. He'd skipped his classes to drill as a drummer boy with the 3rd Ohio Infantry.

He was happy he had a place to live, but sometimes he hated going home. There were so many people in the house. When he complained about it being too crowded, his parents reminded him that they were there to help his aunt. When his uncle had died more than ten years ago, before Johnny was even born in that very house, his aunt was left to care for their six children. So Johnny's ma and pa went to live with her to help out.

He had a good life, even though he had to share a room with his eight-year-old sister and six-year-old brother. His aunt and cousins treated him fine. He couldn't complain about that, either. He just wanted *more*.

His folks were always busy with the farm, so he barely saw them. It was the way they made their living, after all. Their days began when the sun came up and ended when it went down, so he had more freedom than most boys his age.

Johnny hurried up the drive to the house. He tried to sneak inside, but was stopped by his pa, sitting at the long kitchen table. "Come here, Son."

Had he found out Johnny skipped school today? Was he angry? He didn't look angry. He looked sad and it puzzled Johnny.

His pa waved for Johnny to join him. Once he was seated, his father said, "I'm afraid I have some bad news."

Roman Clem put his hands on his son's shoulders and looked into his eyes. "Your ma is…gone."

Johnny blinked, unsure what his pa was trying to tell him. "What do you mean gone?" *Something happened to her gone? Or she left us gone? I saw sadness in her eyes more than once when she didn't know I was looking. Maybe she ran away?*

"There was an accident." His father turned and sniffed. "She didn't make it," he said when he faced Johnny again.

"What kind of accident?" Johnny's lips trembled. His pa looked sadder than he'd ever seen him.

"She was crossing Railroad Street when the cart got stuck on the train tracks. She tried to get it free, to save the vegetables, when…" He shook his head and swiped at the tears leaking from his eyes before he said, "…the train came. She musta been so set on saving our produce, she didn't see it coming. The cart hit her and threw her across the tracks." He stopped speaking, as though he could see it happening in his mind's eye.

Johnny felt a sadness rise in him that he'd never felt before. His insides bucked and churned, like he was going to throw up. Tears filled his eyes. He flung himself into his father's arms and sobbed. He cried like he'd never cried before. His ma was dead. What would happen to his family now?

*

Johnny stood silent with his father, aunt, cousins and siblings in the cemetery on the outskirts of town. He watched the pine box holding his mother's body lower into the hole in the ground. The emptiness in his soul was like that feeling you get in your stomach when you haven't eaten in a long time.

Preacher Harris's hand dropped onto Johnny's shoulder. "I'm sorry, Son. Your ma was a fine woman."

"Thank you, Sir." Johnny tried to keep his voice from cracking, but failed.

Mrs. Harris leaned down in front of Johnny and put her hands on his face. The sadness in her eyes was almost his undoing, but he remained steady. "You'll be fine, Johnny. Your pa and your aunt will see to it."

He didn't forget the manners his mother had instilled in him. "Thank you, Ma'am. I'm grateful for yours and Preacher Harris's help." They and the church had, after all, arranged for the burial.

She kissed both his cheeks then stepped back and took her husband's proffered elbow.

"You ready to go home, Son?" his father asked.

Johnny shook his head. "Can I stay a few more minutes? To say goodbye for the last time?"

His father nodded, as though unable to speak in his sadness. He cleared his throat. "Come straight home when you're done."

Johnny sniffed and stepped closer to the open grave. He stared down at the coarse box that held the remains of his mother. He swiped away unwanted tears. He had to be strong and took a deep breath to compose himself. "I'm sorry I wasn't a better son," he said through trembling lips. "I never meant to cause you misery by running off and making you worry. And not looking after Mary and Louis when you asked." He paused, uncertain what else to say. "You were a good Ma. I'm sorry I didn't tell you that when I had a chance." He sniffed and swiped at his eyes again. "I love you Ma. I'll miss you more than you know."

With a last goodbye and a heavy heart, he shoved his hands into his pockets and turned toward town.

Newark, Ohio, July 1862

It was hot outside, but Johnny sat in the shade in front of the general store. His legs swung back and forth over the edge of the sidewalk as he reflected on how much his life had changed in the year since his mother died.

His father had remarried. Johnny hated the woman. Well, hate was a strong word. Maybe just disliked her. A lot. He wished his father hadn't married her. He'd told Johnny, Mary Elizabeth, and Louis they needed a mother. She was it. He'd even promised they'd be a family again with a house of their own. But that was mostly because his new bride had refused to live with his aunt. Not because it was what his father wanted.

Now they lived in town. Johnny missed the country and his ma. Especially since his new stepmother doted on Mary Elizabeth and Louis. For all she cared, Johnny didn't even exist. And she tried to put him to work at every turn.

"He's big enough to do more chores," she told his father more than once. The more Johnny did, the less she had to do. It was when he heard her say those things that Johnny sneaked away to spend even more time with the 3rd.

He closed his eyes. Anger filled him, recalling when he'd gone to the 3rd Ohio and asked to join up. He was with them most days anyway. Until he realized he wasn't wanted there anymore than he was at home.

They'd laughed at him when he told them what he wanted to do.

"We don't enlist infants," Leonidas McDougal, the commanding officer, told him.

"I'd be a good drummer boy. I know the beats," Johnny had countered. He'd picked up the drum the men from the 3rd had given him when he first started practicing with their company. He drummed some of the familiar beats. "I drill all the time. You know I do. You wave at me when I'm on the field," he reminded McDougal when he quit.

"It makes no difference, Son. You're too young. Go home and wait till you grow up some." McDougal had turned and walked away without a backward glance, shaking his head and chuckling under his breath.

That memory still burned in Johnny's gut. He pursed his lips and opened his eyes. He was sweating, not sure whether it was from anger, or because the shade had moved.

He was getting up when two old-timers sat down on the bench behind him. Their voices carried, and he couldn't help but hear what they were saying. He sat down again.

Johnny hadn't had much interest in the War of the Rebellion when it started. Ma had told him some of the southern states decided they didn't want to be a part of the United States anymore. Some of them had even withdrawn their allegiance to the country, or seceded, she'd explained to him when he didn't understand. Then in April of '61, Fort Sumter in South Carolina, filled with Federal soldiers, was attacked and a war started. Everybody, even Ma, had said it wouldn't last long. They'd been wrong. The war had been going on for over a year now.

Curious about what the men had to say, Johnny listened.

"I told you this war was gonna last a lot longer than ever'body thought, Sam. Lots of folks believed them boys down south were nothing but peacocks. They're fighters and they've proven it by winning every battle we've fought so far. It's gonna be a long war, I tell you. A long one."

"How long you think it'll go, Joe?" the man named Sam asked.

"Don't know. Might be years more."

"Years?" Sam drawled out.

"Mark my words. It'll be years," Joe replied. "From all I hear, those southern boys will fight until there isn't anything left to fight with. The north has all the factories to make weapons, uniforms and shoes. All the south has is cotton and determination. Time will prove they can't hold on forever, no matter how good of fighters they are. The lack of, well, everything needed to fight a war will be the end of them. They don't have the men to replace the ones killed and the inability to make weapons will drive them into surrendering."

The two men fell silent for a few moments before Joe continued. "Word is a newly forming Michigan regiment is marching through Newark in a couple of days."

"Recruiting?" Sam asked.

"That'd be my guess," Joe replied.

Johnny's chin snapped up. Recruiting? Maybe the Michigan regiment would take him? He'd enlist when they came into town. He'd fight those southerners trying to break up the United States. That was what he'd do. He wouldn't have to stay where he wasn't wanted any longer.

*

Every day Johnny walked up and down Newark's Main Street, waiting for the Michigan regiment to show up. Every day he got more worried the old-timer was mistaken and they weren't coming at all.

A week later, standing outside the general store where he'd first heard the old coots talking about the regiment's arrival, he had his first sight of them coming up the street.

Johnny stepped to the support pole at the edge of the sidewalk, wrapped his arm around it, and waited for the company to make its way toward him. The soldiers, five across, tried to march in time with each other. They didn't succeed. It was obvious, even to him, this new regiment had a lot of work to do to learn how to march together.

At the front of the men, the commander rode a fine black horse. The plume in his hat waved in the breeze. Back stiff, he stared straight ahead, never looking at the pretty girls gathered on the sidewalks, waving handkerchiefs and shouting endearments at him. He was a soldier through and through and Johnny studied him with admiration and respect.

As the commander passed, he turned his head ever so slightly toward Johnny. It was so fast Johnny wasn't even sure it happened. A wink. Just for him.

Then and there, Johnny knew he'd made the right decision. As soon as the parade was over, he'd sign up. And that was that.

Johnny followed the regiment to where they made camp. He stopped the first man he came upon and asked, "Where do I go to sign up?"

The soldier laughed in his face. "Boy, you're still wet behind the ears. Come back in a few years." He strolled away sniggering.

Memories of Leonidas McDougal flooded Johnny's mind. He heaved in a deep breath. Whatever it took, he would do this.

Johnny went to the next soldier he found and the next. Each one had the same reaction as the first. "You're too young." "Come back in a few years." "Stupid, snot-nosed kid."

Johnny was determined and changed his strategy. "Where can I find the commander of this regiment?" he asked another man instead.

The soldier eyed him a moment then pointed the way.

Johnny thanked him and started toward a large tent. It was the only one erected as yet. An American flag fluttered atop it.

He was stopped by two soldiers when he tried to enter.

"State your business, Son. Nobody goes in without permission. Not even a boy."

"I want to enlist."

Both soldiers chuckled.

"Son, hasn't anyone told you you're too young to enlist?"

Heat crept up Johnny's neck. Too many people had told him exactly that too many times. Nobody was taking him seriously, and he was as serious as apoplexy!

"I want to join up as a drummer boy. I have my own drum. I know all the beats." He felt his composure slip, but he stood calm and steady, just like he swore he would on the field of battle.

At that moment the commander, the same man that had winked at him, stepped through the flap. "Is there a problem?" he asked the two sentries.

The men snapped to attention. "No, Sir!"

"Then what is going on?"

"This, er, boy came to enlist," one guard said.

"Enlist?" There was humor in the commander's tone. He took a good look at Johnny and nodded. "I remember you. You seemed pretty impressed by our parade into town earlier."

"Yes, Sir." Johnny snapped his feet together like he'd seen the soldiers of the 3rd do in the presence of an officer. He saluted as they'd done. "That was me, Sir." He studied the black-haired man with a deep receding hairline. His well-trimmed beard had streaks of gray. His eyebrows were thick, his eyes dark and piercing.

With a twist of his lips, the commander flicked a quick return salute. "Let him pass." He stepped aside, waved Johnny inside the tent, and pointed to a chair. "Please. Sit."

Johnny sat.

"Now what is it I can do for you?" He paused. "What's your name, Son?"

"I'm Johnny, John, Clem." He tried to sound older than he was, hoping the man wouldn't ask his age.

The commander stuck out his hand. "I'm pleased to meet you, Johnny, John, Clem," he corrected. "I'm Colonel Moses Wisner, commander of the soon to be mustered 22nd Michigan Volunteer Infantry."

"I'm pleased to meet you, Sir." Johnny shook his hand.

A huge smile lit Johnny's face. This man was taking him seriously.

"What can I do for you?" the colonel asked.

"I want to join up. Enlist. As a drummer boy," Johnny added. He knew most drummer boys were young.

"And why do you want to do that?"

Johnny pursed his lips in thought. He wanted to say the right thing. "I want to do my duty. To stop the Rebs from splitting the Union." His shoulders stiffened with pride.

The Colonel smiled and sat back in his chair. He studied Johnny a moment then asked, "How old are you, John?"

Johnny squared his shoulders. "Eleven in three weeks."

The colonel heaved a heavy sigh. He leaned forward again and crossed his hands on his lap. "I'm sorry, but you're too young to enlist. We just can't take someone your age. Even to drum. I am sorry."

"But—"

The colonel lifted his hand, cutting off Johnny's retort. "There's nothing I can do." He stood and called out to the sentries. "Show this young man home." He turned to Johnny, offered his hand again and said, "I am sorry." Without giving him a chance to argue, Johnny was ushered from the tent.

Johnny didn't care *who* told him he couldn't join the regiment. His mind was set. He sneaked inside his house and gathered a few things to take with him. An extra shirt, trousers and underwear, an old pair of shoes that were too small but might be useful someday. A metal plate and cup, utensils, and a hat to keep the sun off his head.

He found an old gum blanket of his fathers to wrap it all in. The blanket would come in handy to ward off the rain if he had to sleep outside. He was thankful it was summer, so he didn't have to worry about the weather turning cold. At least not for a while.

With his few belongings, he sneaked back out and headed to the camp outside town. More tents had been erected, so he hunkered down a little way away from the ones on the edge. And waited.

Until he got hungry.

He rifled through his bag to find the biscuits he'd put inside. The ones his stepmother had made for supper tonight. Maybe she wouldn't miss them. If she did, she'd probably miss them more than she would him.

He thought about his ma. He still grieved for her. Things had changed so much since she died. Johnny sniffed. That's when he smelled it. Food cooking.

He looked at the few biscuits in his pack and decided he'd try to get his hands on some of the soldiers' food. He was sure they had plenty and wouldn't notice if some was gone.

He followed his nose to where a man was hunched in front of a fire. Several pans sat on rocks in the middle of the stone circle. Each pan popped with three or four slabs of salted beef or pork.

It smelled like Heaven.

Johnny's mouth watered. His stomach growled. He had to have some. But it was dangerous. If they caught him, what might they do to him? He wasn't normally a thief, but he *was* hungry. He bit his lip and pondered the situation. They'd already told him to go away. How many times would they tell him before they got mad?

The man cooking was big with a beard and mustache that matched his brown hair. Gray peppered his temples. His eyes looked brown too.

Every so often the man walked away. The next time he did, Johnny would grab a piece or two of the meat, a couple wafers of hard tack, and run.

He got his chance a few minutes later when the man left the meat unattended. Johnny rushed over, grabbed a handful of hard tack and reached for the meat, but couldn't pick it up out of the pan. He looked around for something to wrap it in, when he felt a cold gun barrel on his neck.

"Don't do it," the man hissed from behind.

Johnny fell forward, then rolled to his backside, and stared up at the angry man.

Surprise filled the soldier's face. "You."

Johnny was looking at the first soldier who had laughed at him when he told him he wanted to enlist.

The soldier dropped the musket, grabbed Johnny by his shirt collar and hauled him to his feet.

Several other soldiers joined the first, until eight or ten men stood gawking at Johnny.

"What's this, Harve? When you called us for chow, we didn't expect to find you reeling in this little fish." One of the men chuckled.

"He's too small to do anything with. You gonna throw him back for trying to steal our food?" asked another with a gleam in his eyes.

Humiliation tore through Johnny. He might be young, but he knew when he was being mocked. He struggled against the man who had a tight grip on his shirt.

"Stop wriggling you little varmint," the man said.

Johnny stilled, but only for a moment.

"What're you doing here, boy?" the soldier the others had called Harve drawled.

Johnny stopped struggling and stiffened his back. "What did it look like I was doing? I was going to take some food. I'm hungry." He glared at them as though they were the stupidest men on the planet.

"You got some real gumption, boy," another of the men drawled. "We could have you shot for stealing." He poked Johnny in the belly.

"Aw, leave the kid alone," Harve told the others. He released Johnny's shirt. "If you're that hungry, pull up some dirt. We'll share what we got."

Johhny's eyes got wide. "You will?" He couldn't believe his luck.

"Sure, why not. How much could a little fish like you eat?" Harve guffawed at his own joke.

Johnny felt his face flame, but he kept his mouth shut. Humiliation was way better than hunger.

"We ain't got no extra plates or utensils for the boy," one man said.

"I got a plate. And utensils." Johnny ran to where his pack was hidden, pulled out the necessary knife and fork, then hurried back. The men hooted with laughter when he returned ready to eat.

"Come on, boy. Let's get you fixed up." Harve took Johnny's plate and put a slab of pork, a few beans, and a piece of softened hard tack on it. Johnny picked up the plate, ready to dig in when Harve stopped him. "Wait."

Puzzled, Johnny waited.

"I'm gonna show you how to make skillygalee."

"Skilly ga what?"

"Skillygalee. Watch. And learn." Harve took Johnny's piece of softened hard tack and laid the slab of pork on it. "Skillygalee." Harve grinned.

Johnny picked up the concoction and bit into it. Most of the hard tack crumbled onto his plate.

"It's still hard tack. Sometimes even soaking it in water isn't enough to soften it," Harve told him with a wink.

It didn't matter, it filled Johnny's hungry belly.

He sat around the fire with the soldiers, listening to them talk about Colonel Wisner's recruiting efforts for the 22nd Michigan Volunteer Infantry regiment. Where they'd been and where they were going. He felt like one of them, until the men left for their own tents or gathered to play cards or dice elsewhere.

Johnny got up and started toward the trees where his pack and drum were hidden. And the gum blanket he'd sleep under tonight.

"Hold up, Johnny," Harve said. "Where you headed?"

Johnny shrugged and pointed into the woods. "I got no place to go," he lied.

"Where you from?" Harve questioned.

"Uh, Zanesville," he fibbed again. He didn't want anyone to know he was from Newark, so close to here. Zanesville was about twenty-five miles away. If Harve thought that was too far, maybe he wouldn't try to send him back. Especially not with night coming.

"Did you run away?"

Johnny shrugged and nodded. "My ma died a year ago. Things haven't been the same since. So, I left." He swallowed. It was the truth. Just not the whole truth.

"What about your pa?"

Johnny shrugged. "He won't miss me. He's busy with his new wife."

"Ah," Harve said as though he understood everything now.

"Come on, kid. It's too late to send you anywhere today. You can bunk with me tonight."

Johnny hesitated. He couldn't leave his pack and drum in the woods.

"What's the matter?" Harve asked.

"I, uh, my stuff is in the woods."

"Well, come on then. Let's go get it and get you settled. At least for tonight." Harve started toward where Johnny pointed, Johnny quick on his heels.

The next day Harve tried to send Johnny home. "We're shipping out soon. You gotta go."

"I don't want to. I want to stay here. I can drum. I'll show you." Johnny grabbed his drum and tapped out the beats he'd learned with the Ohio 3rd.

Harve stopped him halfway through and Johnny was certain he was going to be turned away again.

"What if we send a telegram to your pa to come and get you?"

"I'll run away again. Please. Don't send me back. I want to stay. I want to be a soldier."

Harve sighed heavily. "I guess somewhere along the line we'll need to recruit a drummer boy. Why not you?" He raised his eyebrows. "I gotta let the colonel know, though. If he says no..."

"I still won't go. I'll follow."

"You're that determined?"

Johnny nodded furiously.

Johnny never knew whether Harve told the colonel about him or if the colonel agreed to let him stay. One night turned into days then days into weeks.

Every morning Johnny asked to be taught something new in a soldier's routine. He learned how to cook the salt beef and pork the men got daily while in camp. Once in a while, they got fresh vegetables when they stopped en route to wherever it was they were going. The fresh produce made him think of his old life. But this was his new life. The one he'd chosen.

Once, they camped near an orchard and had fried apples wrapped in the softened hard tack, then cooked over the fire. It wasn't pretty, but it was sweet and as close to apple pie as they could get.

They traveled for nearly a month before they reached Pontiac, Michigan. On August 29th, the regiment was mustered into service as the 22nd Michigan Volunteer Infantry Regiment of the United States.

"We're taking out in the morning, Johnny," Harve said when the two were turning in of an evening in early September.

"Where we headed?" Johnny asked, anxious to be on the move again.

"Scuttlebutt is that we're headed for Lexington."

"Lexington?" Johnny wasn't so good with geography.

Harve must have seen Johnny's confusion. "That's in Kentucky," he explained. "It's a very long way from here. Word is we'll go by rail and boat to get there." He paused then added, "I hear we're only a few men shy of a thousand in the regiment." He grinned and chucked Johnny under the chin. "Not including you."

Johnny said nothing. He *wished* he was included in the rolls, but thankful he hadn't been sent away. He had a place to sleep, food to eat, and he was learning to be a soldier. What more could a boy want?

September 4, 1862

Johnny got up early to help Harve cook breakfast. He'd been with the regiment for a little over a month now and felt comfortable around the men. Most of them treated him like a kid brother. They ruffled his hair and slapped him on the back. Some even acted as though they respected him.

"Johnny! Johnny, come over here." Harve waved from a short distance away for Johnny to come at the double-quick.

Johnny skidded to a stop beside his friend. They were in front of the Pontiac train depot at the edge of town, not far from the fairgrounds where they were camped. "What?"

Harve pointed at the platform, a silly grin on his face.

Johnny frowned. "It's a bunch of ladies talking to Colonel Wisner."

Harve nodded several times, that goofy grin still on his face. "Pretty ladies. Lots and lots of pretty ladies."

Johnny snorted. "You act like you've never seen one before."

Harve snorted back. "Not this many in one place in a long time." His eyes never strayed from the several dozen women in their fancy dresses, wearing white gloves and holding their parasols. Every one smiled and curtsied to the Colonel as he strode past.

"What're they doing?" Johnny was puzzled by their behavior. The only real ladies he knew were the ones in Newark. Ones he saw from a distance and never spoke to.

"Lookie there." Harve pointed. "They've made a stand of colors for the regiment and are presenting it to Colonel Wisner."

"Stand of colors?" Johnny asked, confused.

"A flag. For us to carry into battle," Harve explained.

Understanding now, Johnny turned back to the presentation. The Colonel took one end of the flag and one of the women took the other. When it was unfurled, they lifted it for everyone to see. The motto, embroidered in gold read, "From the Ladies of Pontiac."

The ladies clapped daintily and the soldiers who had gathered whooped and hollered their approval.

"We, the Women's Guild of Pontiac, present this flag to the 22nd Michigan to pledge our solidarity with the cause of the preservation of this Union," the portly, gray-haired spokeswoman called out to the growing crowd.

Everyone clapped and cheered.

"I accept this gracious gift on behalf of the 22nd Michigan. We thank you." Wisner bowed low.

The spokeswoman tilted her head in a courteous nod and curtsied. The women behind her did the same.

Wisner turned and waved at Captain Atkinson.

The captain joined the Colonel and took the other end of the flag from the lady and the two folded it. The Colonel held up the standard and said to his troops, "Boys, this will be with us everywhere we go from now on." He turned to the women, swept off his hat and bowed low again.

The ladies curtsied one last time. "It was our sincere pleasure, Colonel Wisner," the spokeswoman said. She turned, lifted her arms, and the women hurried away.

Wisner handed the flag to Atkinson. "Take care of this. It shall be our standard from here on out." He faced the men. "We leave at noon," he told the gathered troops. They saluted the Colonel, who responded with a salute of his own.

"We leave at noon for Lexington?" Johnny asked Harve as they cleaned then stowed the dirty breakfast crockery. "Why are we going there?"

"I'm just a lowly private, boy. I'm not privy to knowing why we do anything. We just do what we're told and go where they tell us."

*

That afternoon the almost 1000 soldiers of the 22nd Michigan marched to the depot and boarded the train for Detroit. From Detroit later that night, they took a boat to Cleveland. In Cleveland they boarded another train to Cincinnati. At two a.m. on the morning of

September 6th, the regiment ate breakfast supplied by the city of Cincinnati and was issued rations for their upcoming march to Lexington.

Captain Atkinson stepped in front of the men and raised his hands to stop them from dispersing. "Fill your haversacks with whatever food is left, men," he shouted.

Johnny didn't need any incentive to grab as much food as he could. He stuffed biscuits, cornbread, and bacon into his pack with a wide grin on his face.

"Looks like we'll be enjoying this nice meal for a few more days," Harve said.

Johnny didn't answer. He was too busy packing his bag and filling his mouth.

They marched toward Lexington for months, with an occasional skirmish to keep the men alert. Johnny's first taste of battle came on a knoll in the center of a cabbage field outside Covington, Kentucky. It was a quick fight with no injuries. Now that it was over, the men laughingly called it the "Battle of Cabbage Hill." It wasn't so funny when Johnny was in the thick of it, though, drumming his heart out.

They ate cabbage for days afterward, and were happy to have it.

Harve watched over Johnny like he would a son. As the 22nd continued their march toward Lexington, Johnny's respect and admiration for his mentor grew even more. The regiment went from one camp to the next in weather that went from hot to cool, to downright cold.

Camped not far from Lexington, Harve pulled Johnny aside one night after supper. "Forget cleanup for now," he told him. "Boys, gather 'round," he shouted to the men in the company.

When most of the men had gathered, Harve laid his arm across Johnny's shoulders. "This young man has more heart and soul than most grown men I've come across in my thirty years. He does what he's told and more. He makes our lives easier by cooking and doing most anything we ask of him. And he doesn't complain about sleeping on the ground, in the cold, like a lot of you boys do." He raised an eyebrow and looked around the gathered men with a grin.

Heat rushed up Johnny's neck, despite the chill wind. What was Harve about?

"In payment for your unwavering loyalty, we've had something made for you." Harve took a package wrapped in brown paper with a string around it from one of the men.

Johnny studied the package with confusion. Why were they giving him a gift? They'd given him more than he could have ever asked for. A feeling of belonging.

Harve handed him the package. "Take this with our gratitude, Johnny. It's from the whole company."

It got so quiet Johnny heard the wind soughing through the trees. He turned the package over several times before he tore the paper away. And gasped. It was a uniform. Just for him. His lips trembled and he tried to keep tears from forming, but they came anyway.

"I, I…"

"Don't say anything," Harve said to rousing cheers and clapping. When the noise quieted, Harve handed him an envelope. "The uniform isn't all of it."

Johnny shook his head, unable to comprehend what was happening. He took the envelope Harve offered him with a shaking hand. When he opened it, he was sure his eyes would pop right out of his head. He counted the contents. Thirteen dollars. The pay each man here received every month. He lifted teary eyes to Harve.

Before Johnny could speak, Harve said, "You've earned it. And you'll earn it every month from here on out. You now have a uniform like every man here, and you'll get paid the same as we do."

Johnny didn't understand. He wasn't on the rolls. How could he get the same pay every other man got? How had he gotten this beautiful uniform? He lifted questioning eyes to Harve.

Johnny saw the hint of tears in Harve's eyes before the older man swiped them away with a grunt.

Curiosity got the better of Johnny. He had to know. "How did you get this uniform?" he asked.

"Camp followers."

"Huh?" Johnny had no idea what that meant.

"The women who follow us. They do our laundry and mending. Some are wives. Some aren't." A funny look crossed his face and that of the other men before Harve schooled his features and continued. "I went to one of them and asked her to make a uniform for you. She said she'd seen you around camp and knew just what size to make it."

"And the money?" Johnny was dumbfounded by the men's generosity.

Harve shrugged. "We all chipped in. With a hundred men in the company, it wasn't hard to come up with thirteen-dollars. A penny here, a dime there. Even the occasional two bits. And we'll do it again next month and the next and the next," he added with a gleam in his eyes. "As long as we get paid, you'll get paid."

Between his tears, trying to swallow the lump in his throat, and his trembling lips, all Johnny could manage was, "Thank you." He tucked the package under his arm and hurried away, the envelope with the money crushed in his hand. If there was one thing Johnny intended to do, it was earn that thirteen dollars a month.

In the last months, Harve had become his mentor. But he'd become so much more. He was a friend.

Johnny's best friend, teaching him how to be a good soldier and helping him practice his drumming skills.

Johnny learned more with the 22nd than he ever had sneaking away from school and drilling with the 3rd. Every drumbeat meant something different. There was the signal to "meet here" or "retreat." The one he liked best was a long roll, the signal to "attack." Each time he practiced, adrenaline flowed through him, and he felt ten feet tall.

Harve was able to teach him what he needed to know because every man in the command had to learn the beats too. They had to know how to respond when the only thing that could be heard over the noise of battle was the drum.

Johnny had never felt so much a part of anything in his entire life.

They'd been at Camp Ella Bishop in Lexington since the end of October. Johnny learned a brutal fact about the army that winter. When the weather turned cold, many of the men got sick from sleeping on the damp ground, exposed to the elements during picket duty in open fields, and having little shelter from the storms that raged throughout the winter. Colonel Wisner was one of those men who fell ill.

More than once, Johnny questioned his decision to be here as he shivered in his tent. He could have been in Newark in a warm, cozy bed. But he wouldn't have been happy there.

It was the first day of the New Year and the men were sleeping off too much celebration from the night before. After morning mess, Johnny shrugged on the oversized coat the company had gotten for him in Cincinnati. He trudged his way to where Colonel Wisner was convalescing after falling ill. It was déjà vu when two sentries halted him at the door.

"I'd like to see the Colonel. I'm Johnny Clem, the drummer boy from Company C."

"What's your business?"

"I want to pay my respects."

The sentry pursed his lips and nodded. "Let me check with the doctor."

When the man returned, he said, "I'm sorry. The Colonel is highly contagious. He's allowed no visitors."

Johnny's hope deflated. He wanted to thank the Colonel. "Can you get a message to him for me?" he asked.

"Sure," the sentry replied.

"Can you tell him thank you, from me, for not sending me away when I first came?"

"I can do that." The sentry sniggered. "If I recall, you were pretty persistent. I guess the Colonel realized if he sent you away, you'd come right back."

Heat rushed up Johnny's neck and he nodded. "I would have. I wanted to be a soldier and nobody, not even a colonel, was going to stop me." He grinned.

"You succeeded." The sentry paused a moment then said, "I'll be sure to get him your message."

Three days later, on January 4, 1863, Johnny learned that Colonel Moses Wisner had succumbed to typhoid fever and died.

*

"I am Colonel Heber LeFavour," the new commander of the 22nd informed the regiment at muster a few days later. He stood straight as a post, his hands locked behind his back. His uniform was trim, his black boots polished to a high sheen. "It is under sad circumstances I take command, but it is I who is now in charge. Do not be mistaken."

Johnny stood silent, surrounded by the men of Company C. Harve stood stiff beside Johnny, as always his protector.

"Things will be different under my command. Obey orders and we will get along. Dismissed!"

Johnny's heart ached knowing Colonel Wisner had died. He was a good man and well-liked by his men. And what had Colonel LeFavour meant when he said things would be different? Johnny's breath caught when a thought struck him. Would this new colonel send him away?

Day after day Johnny waited for someone to take him to this new colonel to be told he had to go. Weeks passed, yet he remained. He did his duty and was becoming the best drummer boy in the regiment. He intended to give this new colonel no reason to send him away.

The only difficulty was that when he wasn't cooking or practicing, Johnny was bored. The men wouldn't let him play cards or dice with them, so he had nothing to do to occupy his time.

"We've already let you soldier, Johnny. We're not gonna corrupt you too," he was told more than once. What they didn't say was that he was too young and for that, Johnny was glad.

Sometimes the men disappeared for hours at a time. When they came back, they had goofy grins on their faces and smiled for hours afterwards.

"What's wrong with them, Harve?" Johnny would ask. "They look like somebody's tickling them with a feather, but they ain't really laughing."

That same grin lit Harve's face every once in a while. "You'll understand when you grow up. For now, just know the boys are getting a little...relief from their duties."

With nothing else to keep him busy, Johnny stayed in his tent, out of the miserable weather. He polished his belt and boots and slept.

In late February, the regiment marched to Hickman Bridge on the Kentucky River near Danville. They had no sooner rolled up in their blankets in a camp without tents, when a bugle sounded, and they were ordered to return to Lexington. Sometimes, Johnny thought the officers who ran this army were crazy, but he was happy to be moving again. Anything was better than sleeping in the cold on the hard ground in the dead of winter.

It was late March when Colonel LeFavour was thrown from his horse and grievously injured. He was replaced by Lieutenant Colonel Sanborn.

"We depart in two hours," Sanborn told the regiment. "General Pegram and his Confederates are near Danville, we believe, to relieve the depot there of its cache of weapons and ammunition. We must divert them from that mission. Our orders are to intercept them." He paused, twisted his neck as though to relieve pressure there, then continued. "Men, this is going to be a fast, arduous journey. It is forty miles that must be done quickly. Hence, we depart in two hours. Dismissed!"

11 a.m., March 24, 1863, near Danville, Kentucky

In battle formation, Johnny stood with the flag bearers behind the officers at the front of the company awaiting the order to march. His chest hurt with each labored breath. His heart pounded almost as fast as his hands moved when he played his drum. He turned to Harve for courage, standing in line behind him.

The older man smiled and nodded. "You can do this. I haven't seen a better drummer boy in all my days. But stay close to me, you hear?"

Too scared to speak, Johnny nodded and faced front again. He'd seen small skirmishes, but nothing like this. This was going to be a real battle.

In front of the line of men, Lt. Colonel Sanborn lifted his arm, shouted forward, then flung his hand down. The signal to follow the company marching ahead.

Johnny swallowed and began to beat the drum. Slowly, he and the men marched onward. The order to charge was shouted. At the double-quick, he drummed the long roll. The signal to attack.

He ran without missing a beat. They met the enemy. Confederates. Rebels. Johnnies. Men like Harve and the other boys of C Company who had become Johnny's family. A wave of fear washed over him. He thought about running away, but he couldn't let the men down. He'd worked too long and hard to run. He would stay and do his duty no matter what. They needed him. He sucked in a deep breath and kept going, beating his drum. A quiet calm washed over him. With Harve nearby, he charged ahead into the clash of men and steel.

He'd never imagined it would be like this. It took all he had to keep his hands steady and not miss any beats.

The men surged forward.

He rushed ahead with them.

Harve fought like a wild man beside him, bent on his own survival and protecting Johnny. One minute he was there. The next he was gone.

Johnny scoured the field around him to find his friend. Had Harve fallen and Johnny didn't see it happen? Was he injured or dead? How would Johnny know? The questions rattled in Johnny's head until he felt sick and alone as men clashed around him with bayonets and muskets.

As the battle progressed, despite his fear for Harve, Johnny remembered his duties and performed them well. When he stopped drumming, he was to search for wounded soldiers and help them from the field. Maybe one of those soldiers would be Harve. Sometimes he had to call for assistance. Other times he would act as a stretcher bearer with other drummers to get an injured man to the medical tent.

He had no idea how long he searched the field for wounded, and Harve, or how long the battle raged before the order to retreat was issued.

Johnny drummed his heart out so the men around him knew to fall back. With a few drumbeats, the regiment began its retreat to Hickman's Bridge.

It had been a day of more fighting than Johnny had ever seen. He was glad it was over. If he had a choice, he'd never fight another battle again. But he wouldn't shirk his duties. He'd given his word to the men of Company C and he intended to do it. Until he couldn't.

Rejoining the rest of the men, Johnny was hauled off his feet and swung in a circle. "You're alive!" Harve shouted.

"So are you," Johnny cried out when he was dropped to his feet. Unashamed of his show of emotion, Johnny grabbed his friend around the waist, buried his head in his chest and hugged him. "I was so scared," he said, his voice muffled. "You were there and then you weren't."

"The fighting got too hot around you, so I led those Johnnie Rebs away." Harve stepped back and chucked Johnny under the chin. "Hope you don't mind." He flashed a mischievous grin.

Johnny wagged his head back and forth. "No siree, I don't. I wondered why the fighting thinned." He chuckled. "Guess they were hightailing it after you. Weren't worried about a little drummer boy," he added with a tilt of his head. Affection and devotion for this man swelled inside him. Harve was willing to die for him. He'd more than proven that.

Johnny sobered. He'd been lucky today. He was a boy, but he'd heard many times that lots of drummer boys had died on the field of battle throughout this war. Some shot, some killed in explosions or random musket fire. He was determined not to become one of them.

From Hickman's Bridge the regiment marched to Stanford then Lebanon. They arrived in Nashville, Tennessee, the evening of the 13th of April.

A couple weeks after their arrival in Nashville, Harve pulled Johnny aside. "I got something for you."

Johnny shook his head. What else could Harve possibly give him? When the older man pulled a musket with a shortened barrel from behind his back, Johnny was speechless. Again. He looked up at his friend and mentor with affection.

"I been working on it since Danville. You need to be able to defend yourself. Can't beat off a Reb with a drum stick," Harve said with a smirk. Before Johnny could interrupt, he added. "And if something happens to me..."

Johnny didn't want to think about that. "You, you can't." He couldn't say anything more.

"I know. It'll be fine. We haven't seen that much fighting, so maybe we'll get through this war with our skin on. Don't worry about nothing. I don't plan to go to my Maker anytime soon."

Johnny swallowed and nodded. He'd be happy if they never went into battle again. Still, he practiced defending himself every day. Just in case.

Johnny slept with his musket beside him. It went everywhere he went. He fashioned a sling and sheath to carry it while he drummed. Aside from his uniform and his thirteen dollars a month, it was the best present he'd ever gotten.

The regiment remained in camp at Nashville until early September. It was almost five months of guard duty for the men and boredom for Johnny. But after the clash at Danville, he was happy for as much boredom as he could get.

On September 5th, once again under the command of Colonel LeFavour, the regiment started for Chattanooga, Tennessee. Day and night they marched, carrying all their equipment, arriving at Bridgeport, Alabama, on the 11th of September. They camped on Seven Mile Island until the morning of September 13th, when they left for Rossville, Georgia. The regiment arrived in Chattanooga on the 14th, bone-weary, asleep on their feet, after the long, forty-mile march.

Johnny was so beat when they arrived early that afternoon, he didn't even care that he was hungry. He tossed out his bedroll, curled up on it, and was asleep in seconds.

Three days later, after a brief but harmless meeting with the enemy while reconnoitering the area around Ringgold, the 22nd was back in Rossville.

It was barely morning when an explosion rocked the earth under Johnny. He nearly jumped out of his skin. He did jump out of his bedroll.

"What was that?" he screamed, his hands fisted. He knew the sound of shelling, but it was usually from a distance. These sounded, and felt, like they'd landed not fifty feet away.

Harve grabbed Johnny by the shoulders and shook him. "Get your boots on. The Rebs are bombarding camp."

Johnny didn't need to be told twice. His boots were on in the matter of seconds. Men ran, shouted orders, grabbed muskets, and rushed to the perimeter of camp to meet the enemy.

Another shell exploded nearby. Johnny went to the ground, shaking like a leaf in a windstorm.

Harve dropped to his knees beside him. "Get behind that tree and stay there," he commanded.

Johnny didn't hesitate. He got to his feet, ran to the tree, and hugged it.

The men, including Harve, charged from camp.

It wasn't long before they returned.

Johnny hurried to Harve when he spotted him. "What happened?"

"They ran," Harve told him. "Didn't take much, just a bit of push back and they tucked tail and ran."

"Well, I'm glad of it," Johnny said. "I've had a belly full of Rebs. The less I see, the better."

"Spoken like a man who's seen his share of battle," Harve said with a chuckle.

"I've seen enough. If I never saw anymore, I'd be happy."

Harve clapped Johnny on the back and led him to his bedroll. "Get some sleep. No telling how long before we'll be called up again."

Johnny didn't argue. He flopped down on the blankets and was asleep again in minutes.

The next morning began like any other day in camp. Harve and Johnny cooked the men's breakfast rations then sat around talking, waiting for orders, their gear packed and ready.

"We gonna see a fight?" Johnny asked Harve.

His friend sucked in a deep breath and nodded. "Now that we're attached to Rosecrans's army, it looks like we will. Seems Braxton Bragg wants to retake Chattanooga. It hasn't been long since him and his Rebs were booted out by General Rosecrans, but Bragg wants Chattanooga back. Word is he's headed north toward the city."

"And we're gonna stop him?" A lump formed in Johnny's throat.

"Scuttlebutt is that Rosecrans has sixty-thousand men intending to do just that. We'd best be ready to move out at a moment's notice." Harve ruffled Johnny's hair. Johnny hated it when Harve or the other men did that. It made him feel like a baby, but he let his friend get away with it. Maybe Harve was nervous about the coming fight too?

When Harve saw the look Johnny gave him, he sighed and said, "All right. I won't do it no more."

There was a gleam in his eyes when he said it. Johnny didn't believe it for a minute.

It was one o'clock that afternoon when Colonel LeFavour brought the order himself.

"Men, we've been ordered to march."

Johnny suppressed the fear that zipped through him. He'd signed up for this. It was his job and he meant to do it. He sucked in a deep breath to calm his nerves, gathered his drum and musket, and followed Harve and the men of Company C out of camp.

The 22nd was positioned on the left side of the road, the 89th on the right. The 18th Ohio Battery was on the road to the rear of the other two. A large field loomed ahead with a log cabin on the far perimeter and what looked like a creek with thick brush and timber around it.

Johnny opened his mouth to ask Harve if he knew where they were, when musket fire exploded in front of him. He went to his belly with the other men as bullets whizzed around them.

The barrage continued until the Federal battery fired upon the log cabin. A direct hit sent the Johnny Rebs scurrying from the house as debris fell around them.

Johnny watched with satisfaction as the enemy hurried toward the creek and disappeared in the brush and trees.

"That was easy," Johnny said with a smile when he got to his feet. "I could get used to having a Battery nearby."

"I could too," Harve said with a grin. "Makes those Johnny Rebs think twice about getting close."

The regiment bedded down in the field. What was left of the cabin became the Federal headquarters.

Johnny moaned when he realized all their gear had been left behind. They had to sleep on the ground using their arms for pillows with no tents and no blankets. The night was cold. Curling into a ball, Johnny thought it would never end.

Unable to sleep, Johnny wandered, and ran smack into General Rosecrans himself.

"I'm, I'm so sorry, Sir. I..."

The General lifted his hand for silence. "Apparently, you couldn't sleep either."

"No, Sir. It's a mighty cold night and, well, I can't stop thinking about tomorrow."

"You and me both," the General commented with a smile. He studied Johnny in the moonlight. "Are you that drummer boy I've been hearing about?" he asked.

"From Company C, Sir. I hope it's good things you've heard," Johnny said in a rush.

"Indeed, it has." Rosecrans paused in thought a moment then said, "If you ever find yourself in the same place I am, come see me." He stepped away. "Get some sleep. You're going to need it." He turned on his heel and disappeared.

Sunday morning, the 20th of September, broke bright and beautiful. Johnny and Harve were hunched over the morning fire cooking the day's rations. Bacon sizzled and hardtack was being softened for skillygalee. Johnny jerked upright when artillery boomed in the distance. "That was close," he told Harve, squatted beside him.

"It was." Harve had no sooner spoken when bugles sounded for the men to fall in. He grabbed his and Johnny's guns.

Johnny threw his drum strap over his head. He took his musket from Harve and shoved it into the sheath on his side.

A second lieutenant, replacing Captain Atkinson while he was away, rode up and addressed the men. "Our orders are to advance to the front in support of General Thomas."

"What about breakfast?" a heavyset soldier asked.

"If you haven't already eaten, there'll be none. We march. Now!"

The boys of Company C scrambled for the last of their equipment. Some speared the half-cooked bacon on their bayonets.

"That's not such a bad idea," Harve told Johnny. "Maybe we won't go far and will have a chance to finish cooking it later. I'll spear some for us."

Harve had barely a moment to stab the bacon before the men fell in and began to march.

It didn't take long to realize there would be no stopping to cook the bacon, let alone eat it, or anything else for that matter. They were headed into battle. With a grumbling stomach and a complaint on his lips, Harve, along with the rest of the men, tossed their uncooked bacon away.

Johnny worked his way through heavy brush, careful to keep his drum from being impaled by a tree limb or heavy thicket. When they came out of the bushes, he stopped in his tracks. The sight of dead men lying in the grass outside the buildings and barns of the farmstead ahead made his stomach churn. "They're everywhere, Harve," Johnny barely whispered.

"Looks like they used this place yesterday as a hospital." Harve gave a solemn nod. Artillery, musket and rifle fire exploded not far away. "Seems like those Johnnies are trying to keep us from joining up with General Thomas." He gazed out across the field where shells exploded.

Johnny's heart pounded like the artillery in the distance. "And we're gonna be in the thick of it." He swallowed the lump that had formed in his throat again.

"We're not going anywhere until we're told, so drop your drum and take a breath."

Harve's stomach growled, reminding Johnny he was hungry too. "Sure wish we had that bacon back." Johnny sighed.

Harve frowned and nodded. "Me too. Right now, all we can do is wait for further orders. And help," he added, waving his arm at the dead.

As he helped with the burial detail, Johnny pondered the men's stories. Did they have mothers and fathers, sisters and brothers who would mourn them? If *he* fell, would his family ever know what happened to him?

Unwilling to think on it any longer, he lay back and closed his eyes. Although hungry, Johnny was happy for the respite.

About two o'clock Colonel LeFavour addressed the men. "We're to go up Horseshoe Ridge and join the Federal line to the right of General Brannan's division. The 89th Ohio will form to our right." He searched the faces of his men. "God's speed."

Company C reached Horseshoe Ridge at two-thirty and formed behind the companies already in position.

Johnny slid his drum around to his back and went to his belly like the rest of the men. He kept his eyes open wide. Longstreet's Confederates were supposedly coming straight at them, although Johnny couldn't see them over the rise of the hill in front of him.

"Check your loads," LeFavour told his men as he walked among them. "Select your man and aim for the heart. Stand firm and use cold steel."

A chill ran up Johnny's spine at LeFavour's words. That meant there could be bayonets and close contact fighting. As Harve affixed his bayonet, Johnny asked him, "Did you check your load like the Colonel said?"

Harve nodded and patted the ammo box on his belt. "I got forty rounds in here. Forty in my trousers, and my rifle has a full load." He jingled the bullets in his pocket. There was a gleam in his eyes when he added, "Sure hope I got enough."

"More'n eighty rounds better be enough," Johnny said. "If not, we're in for a really bad fight."

Harve ruffled Johnny's hair. "Let's hope I only need twenty."

Johnny frowned and nodded.

The men of the 22nd Michigan held until the Rebels charged. The screech of that damnable Rebel Yell sent goose shivers chasing up and down Johnny's arms. He slid the drum strap around his neck and, as soon as the Colonel shouted the order to fire, got to his feet and beat the drum with a fury.

The companies ahead of him charged forward, but buckled almost immediately from the withering Rebel fire. Men and officers dropped to the ground as bullets flew from every direction. Fear tore through Johnny, but he forced himself to remain calm. He turned to Harve who nodded in a silent bid for him to stay strong.

Up ahead, Johnny spotted the regimental flag the ladies had given to them the day they left Pontiac. The one they'd carried with them every day since. It flapped proudly in the breeze. Until the flag bearer fell to his back. A red flower of blood spread across his chest where a load of grape shot struck him.

Johnny beat his drum and watched the flag hoisted a second time. The man waved the standard back and forth until he, too, fell.

"Stay back, Johnny," Harve told him. "No need for you to rush into that. We'll hear the drum from where you are."

Johnny opened his mouth to argue, but snapped it shut with the look Harve gave him. "Not today, Johnny. Do as I say and you'll see tonight."

Harve turned and rushed into the fray with the other men of Company C.

Johnny beat a long drumroll as Harve and the company charged. Near the front of the lines, the flag fell a third time when a shell exploded nearby.

Johnny drummed.

The standard was raised again.

Johnny lost track of how many times the flag fell and was picked up again. Was it five? Six? Or more?

"Do not falter, men!" LeFavour shouted. "They're falling back."

Johnny was beginning to worry about Harve, when the man dropped to his knees beside him.

"Harve," Johnny cried out, never so happy to see anyone. "You're alive!"

Harve nodded and wiped blood from his hands on his trousers. "Barely." He lifted the tail of his shirt to expose what looked like a bayonet wound.

Johnny gasped.

"It's just a scratch." Harve winked. "I'll be all right. That is if we hold out." He stared out at the fighting ahead of them. "We're out of ammo, Johnny Boy. That eighty rounds I thought was so much is gone. Our flank is exposed and—"

Before Harve finished his sentence, the order to retreat was called. Johnny stood and beat the signal for the men to leave the field. With a grunt, Harve struggled to his feet.

They'd gone only a short distance when Johnny heard the "meet here" order from another drummer.

He picked up the rhythm and charged in that direction. The men followed. When they reached the rendezvous point after six that evening, a courier was conversing with Colonel LeFavour. The message relayed, the courier saluted the colonel, remounted, and wheeled his horse away.

"A new order has been issued," Second Lieutenant Spalding told the men of Company C when they gathered shortly afterward. "General Granger has ordered the 22nd Michigan, 21st and 89th Ohios, to go back up the hill and hold the ground at all hazards. We are to stand firm," he told them. "Additional provisions and reinforcements will follow." Spalding shook his head, as though sorry to give the order and not believing it himself.

There was much grumbling amongst the men, but no one vocalized it to the officers. They gathered their equipment and started up Horseshoe Ridge, as ordered, for the second time that day. When they reached the top, they waited for the promised provisions and reinforcements.

They waited for over an hour. No provisions and no reinforcements came. Thankfully, neither did the Rebs.

Harve shifted to pull out his pocket watch and grimaced. He looked into the sky then down at the watch-face. "It's seven o'clock. The light's fading. Won't be any more fighting today," he told Johnny, relief in his voice.

The words had no sooner left his lips when the Rebel Yell tore through the air from below. The Rebs were charging at the double-quick. Too fast for Johnny to grab his drum. Too fast to do anything but run. He scrambled down the opposite side of the hill and hid behind a clump of bushes. Harve was nowhere to be seen.

Johnny peered through the foliage, unable to tell gray uniform from blue in the dusky darkness.

The clash of men and steel was deafening and seemed to go on forever. Until Johnny heard, "Throw down your arms," in a southern accent. "This here fight is over," came a second, accented command.

The Confederates swarmed the Federals. Even after the Federal troops had ravaged the ammo packs of the dead and equally distributed what they'd found, they were still mostly out of ammunition. The men laid down their weapons when commanded to do so.

Johnny spotted a man riding toward him. He laid down and played dead when the rider stopped in front of him. The man sat a moment, staring down at him before he said, "I know you're alive. I saw you moving before I rode up. It's time to surrender you little Yankee devil."

Johnny had no intention of surrendering. Retreat, yes. Surrender, no. He'd heard the stories about Libby and Andersonville prisons. He would die before he went to either of those places. Grown men died slow, cruel deaths there. What would happen to a boy?

His mind awhirl, he tried to figure out what to do. If he could only...

He used the shadows to turn his body, as though trying to get up, hoping the colonel wouldn't see him pull his musket from under him. He rolled over, lifted the gun and fired.

The colonel yelped and fell from his horse. Johnny didn't know if the man was dead or alive. He didn't care as long as he got away from here. He got to his feet and raced down the hill to join the men who had avoided capture.

With a sick heart, Johnny and the retreating Federals limped their way to Chattanooga. He searched for days, but didn't find Harve with the men who had managed to retreat, regroup, and evade capture. Johnny checked the field hospitals along the way. Harve wasn't with the wounded either. Johnny had to face the truth. Harve was among the many men left upon the battlefield dead or captured.

Although Johnny was with the surviving men of his regiment, he was surrounded by strangers. He was as alone and more scared than he'd ever been in his life.

*

The men in camp at Moccasin Point who had survived the battle didn't stay strangers for long. Johnny regaled the men by showing off his cap. The one, he realized after the battle, that had three bullet holes in it. He told and retold his story about shooting the Confederate Colonel whenever he had the chance and became quite the celebrity.

Shortly after their arrival, Johnny learned that Lieutenant Spalding was among those captured, along with Colonel LeFavour and close to three hundred men. Spalding, although wounded before the last Rebel charge, had refused to leave the field and his men.

Spalding, with the Colonel and other regimental officers, was destined to be shipped to Libby Prison in Virginia at the end of the month. The non-commissioned officers, privates like Harve, would initially go to Libby. But Libby was for officers, so they would be moved to other prisons, including Andersonville, the most hated Confederate prison from all Johnny had heard. Fear washed over him every time he thought about the horrific living conditions there. Exposure to the elements. Lice. Rats. Beatings. Starvation. Death. The thought of his friend being there made him weep.

A few days after their arrival at Moccasin Point, Johnny was called to headquarters. He was met by Major Henry Dean, commanding in LeFavour's absence. The Major stepped up and offered his hand. "Young man, it is my honor to meet you."

Johnny almost fell to the ground. He looked around at the other officers gathered nearby. Each man stood erect with a smile on his face.

"I'm sorry, Sir. I don't understand." Johnny's head was spinning. Why would this officer be honored to meet him? A lowly drummer boy.

After Johnny shook Dean's proffered hand the Major stepped back, snapped his heels together and saluted. The others did the same.

Another officer stepped forward. He had on a double-breasted, dark blue frock coat. The gold buttons had such a high sheen, they glinted in the sunlight coming through the open tent flap. He wore a sash and fringed epaulets on his shoulders.

Johnny stared at the officer a moment before recognition hit. He'd seen the man on the battlefield. It was none other than Major General Thomas himself.

Johnny was at an even bigger loss than when the company had presented him with his uniform and pay.

The general snapped a quick salute then turned to Dean, who handed him what looked like a pair of sergeant's stripes.

Johnny gasped. Those couldn't possibly be for him!

The General stepped closer and bent to look Johnny square in the eyes. "Johnny Clem, for your bravery and fortitude at the recent battle near Chickamauga Creek, please accept this army's sincerest gratitude. You are hereby promoted to sergeant, effective September 20, 1863, the day you proved your courage in battle."

Johnny could only stare at the General and the stripes being offered to him.

With a grin, Thomas stepped back and snapped another brisk salute.

Johnny squared his shoulders and returned the action. He was now a sergeant in Company C of the 22nd Michigan Volunteer Infantry. The magnitude of this promotion wasn't lost on him. Most men didn't achieve this throughout their entire military career. He was twelve.

*

Johnny was starving. His stomach growled. It felt hollow and empty, as though his belly button was scraping his spine.

A week after their arrival at Moccasin Point their rations were cut. Only three-fourths of the men's normal supply of hardtack, bacon and coffee were issued to each man, with no more to be given for four days.

The men and their stomachs grumbled, even as they spent days, that became weeks, building fortifications around camp.

Their defenses didn't keep the Rebs from hurling artillery shells at them. At all hours, day after day, Johnny feared for his life as cannisters were lobbed inside the perimeter. It made for many sleepless nights and frightful days.

Guards returned to camp of a morning with tales of being mocked by Confederate pickets who taunted, "Well, Yank, how do you like Vicksburg?" In reference to the long siege on the Confederate city where the inhabitants had been so hungry, they'd resorted to eating their pets. Even rats.

Johnny took his sergeant's duties seriously, but didn't act superior over anyone. Ever. No longer a drummer boy, especially without the drum he'd lost on the battlefield, he worked beside the men building the fortifications surrounding camp. He grew to know and respect them. But he still missed Harve more than he could have ever guessed. He wondered a hundred times a day whether his friend was still alive and, if he was, how he fared.

From necessity, he forged new friendships among those who didn't resent him for being made a sergeant at such a tender age.

First Week of October 1863

The 22nd was being held in reserve. Perhaps because so many of their men languished in prison camps. Or were dead. They'd lost eighty-five percent of their ranks at Chickamauga. There was no talk of returning to the front, only the assignments of engineering and provost duties, which included building barracks and guard responsibilities.

Johnny was amongst the men assigned to ride into southeastern Tennessee to acquire much needed food supplies for the men at Moccasin Point. He, as much as any of the other men, wanted that train to reach camp with the provisions that would fill their hungry bellies.

After riding two days to acquire the supplies, they were crossing the Sequatchie Valley on their return to Moccasin Point.

Johnny's legs dangled over the tailgate of the wagon he was assigned to protect, his musket gripped tightly in his hands. He sat beside Andy Collins, one of the men from his company who had befriended him. He was a big man with ham-sized hands and a soft heart. Johnny often wondered how he'd come to be a soldier.

Over thirty wagons carrying the much-needed food supplies to the hungry regiment were strung out ahead of and behind Johnny's.

It was a warm day in early October. With the sun beating down on his head, Johnny became drowsy and fell asleep.

Collins nudged him. "Wake up, Sarge. Riders coming."

Johnny jerked awake. Riders meant one thing. Trouble.

He and Collins scurried inside the wagon and tied the tailgate up. Muskets ready, they waited.

Johnny's blood turned to ice when the horsemen came over the ridge. Hundreds of them, racing at breakneck speed toward the wagons. Then came that Rebel Yell that made Johnny tingle with fear.

The brazen Confederates raced by the wagons, shouting and shooting. Johnny fired back, but couldn't hit the fast-moving targets. They had repeating pistols. He and the other guards had one-shot muskets. It was an uneven match from the git-go. He tried to reload, but with the wagon's lurching and pitching, it was impossible.

It wasn't long before they were stopped and surrounded.

"Afternoon, Yanks. Beautiful day for a robbery, ain't it?" one of the riders said in a heavy southern accent to Johnny and Collins. He sat relaxed with one arm across the saddle horn, the other holding a gun on Johnny and Collins. "Y'all are outnumbered and surrounded. Don't do anything foolish and you'll live. Maybe," he drawled. A wicked grin curled his lips. "Drop yer weapons and lift yer hands." He waved his pistol to make sure they complied.

Thoughts of Chickamauga flashed through Johnny's head. Of Harve and Colonel LeFavour and where they were right now. Rotting in Confederate prisons. If they were even still alive. He'd been told to surrender then and refused. This was different though. It wasn't dark. His captor's weapon was in plain sight. And the Reb could fire in a heartbeat—stopping his.

"Do it, Sarge," Collins told Johnny, throwing his spent musket over the tailgate on the ground.

"Sarge?" The Confederate sputtered. "This little squirt is a sergeant?" he repeated with disbelief. Five or six other men had joined him and hooted with laughter. "They must need soldiers awful bad robbin' the cradle like that." He guffawed and waved his gun at Johnny.

Anger ripped through Johnny. He gripped the spent weapon so tightly, his knuckles turned white. He didn't have a choice. He sucked in a deep breath and threw the musket on the ground. The one Harve had made special. Just for him. He might as well have been throwing away a piece of his heart, the pain was so great.

One of the Rebs got off his horse and collected the discarded weapons.

"You boys have the distinction of being captured by General Joe Wheeler," the first rider told Johnny and Collins.

Johnny had heard the name before, spat out like a bad word when he was referred to as "Fighting Joe Wheeler."

"Come on, boy. You ride with me," the first Reb told Johnny. He pointed at Collins. "You kin walk. Tie him up," he told the others.

The last thing Johnny saw before he mounted was Collins's hands being tied. The other end of the rope was lashed to the horn of one of the rider's saddles. Johnny's insides constricted at the thought of what might happen, but there was nothing he could do for Collins or himself.

Johnny always tried so hard to be a man. Right now, all he wanted to do was cry like a little boy.

They'd ridden up and over the hill a short distance when the Reb slowed his horse. They approached what looked to Johnny like the Confederate command center.

"I'd bet my next month's pay General Wheeler will want to meet you. If I thought for one minute, I would *get* paid," the Reb added with a snort.

He walked the horse closer, got off and pulled Johnny down. Johnny stumbled, but stayed upright.

"Come on, Sarge," the Reb drawled disrespectfully. "Let's go meet the General." He dragged

Johnny by the collar of his uniform in front of a table. The man he presumed to be Wheeler stood behind it, studying him curiously. He stroked his dark, well-trimmed beard. His long gray frock-coat was embossed with gold embroidery on the sleeves. The shoulder straps he wore confirmed he was certainly the General.

The soldier shoved Johnny so hard, he had to grab the table to keep from falling.

"This little squirt was guarding one of the supply wagons we captured."

Wheeler's left brow lifted. He leaned over to get face to face with Johnny. "What are you doing here, you damn little Yankee scoundrel?"

Anger zipped through Johnny. He stepped back, stiffened his spine, and squared his shoulders. "I am no more a damn scoundrel than you are...Sir." He stood erect, awaiting the man's reaction.

Wheeler's eyes darkened then he threw his head back and he howled with laughter. When he stopped, he asked, "What's your name, boy?"

"Johnny...John Clem. Sergeant John Clem," he added in a haughty tone, pointing to the stripes on his uniform.

The General stepped around the table, put his arm across Johnny's shoulder, and walked him a few feet away. He turned him to face the men who had gathered since Johnny's arrival.

"This is Johnny Clem, boys." He clapped Johnny on the back. "And I tell you, he's one fighting Yankee baby!"

The men erupted into laughter.

Heat tore through Johnny, but he stood straight and eyed the men laughing at him.

When the men quieted, the General shoved Johnny at the soldier who had brought him into camp. "Take him.

Show our boys what the Union is putting on the field for us to fight."

The soldier saluted and grabbed Johnny's arm. "Let's go, saaarge," he drawled out.

Humiliation and rage coiled inside Johnny. He held his head high as he was paraded through the Confederate camp, taunted and mocked.

"Take off yer uniform," his captor told him.

Johnny's chin jerked up. "If you want it, take it off."

The Reb's eyes lit with the challenge. "You are a brave little cuss, ain't you?" He strode toward Johnny. When he got close enough, Johnny kicked him between the legs.

The man doubled over, writhing in pain. Two soldiers ran up behind Johnny, grabbed his arms, and pinned them behind him.

When his captor could stand, he got in Johnny's face, his body turned so his personal parts couldn't be attacked again. "You little cockroach." He slapped Johnny.

Never in his short life had anyone struck Johnny before. He struggled against the men holding him, but there was no getting free.

"Now...," his captor drawled. "I'll take that coat. And yer hat." His eyes glinted with spite.

Johnny's arms were released long enough to let his captor slide his uniform off. He struggled to keep it, but to no avail.

When his hat was taken, Johnny nearly wrenched his arms out of the sockets fighting to get it back. The man poked his fingers through the three holes, his eyes wide, a wicked grin on his face. "Dang. This boy has seen some shootin'." He sneered at Johnny. "Won't be seein' no shootin' for a long time, boy. All yore gonna see is the inside of a cell." He hooted with laughter.

"Let 'im go, boys," his original captor told the two men holding Johnny. "Let's see what he's got."

Johnny's arms were released and he flew at the man who had stolen his hat. He wrapped his arms around the man's waist and tried to bring him to the ground. The man stepped backward with a grunt. Johnny pummeled his stomach.

The man had the nerve to laugh.

Johnny hit him harder until he was lifted off the ground by his waist, his bottom in the air, his head toward the ground. Johnny kicked and scratched and struggled to get loose. That only caused the men around him to laugh louder.

A moment later he was face down in the dirt.

"Didn't they teach you any manners where you come from...boy?" his captor drawled. "Don't worry, we'll teach you to respect your elders before we're done with you." The man whooped and slapped his comrades on the back.

The man who'd stolen Johnny's hat tossed it to one of the other soldiers who examined it before tossing it to another. Johnny jumped to his feet. "That's mine! Give it back!" He reached for it again and again. Every time he tried to grab it, they lifted it higher then threw it to the next man until Johnny's arms grew tired and he couldn't jump anymore. He stood in the middle of his captors, his chest heaving and glaring with hatred.

Johnny was led to the next camp. "Lookie here, boys," his initial captor shouted. "This is what the Union Army is recruiting these days. Babies! Fighting babies," he quoted General Wheeler. "And a sergeant, no less," he added with disdain. "If that don't beat all."

Laughter filled the air.

Johnny's rage and humiliation warred within him. Rage won. He lashed out whenever he could, catching a Reb who got too close across the cheek with a fist or in the knee with a well-timed kick. It helped assuage his anger, but it didn't help him get away. He was stuck, and there was nothing he could do about it.

Johnny lost track of time during his captivity. Days turned into weeks, possibly months. Each day he was taken from the room or tent where he was held and paraded through the Rebel troops. They laughed and taunted him for his lack of clothing, which they'd stolen, his title of sergeant, and his size, which was small for his age.

"Get up, boy. You're going for a ride," a lieutenant told him when he stepped inside the tent Johnny had been kept in the past few days.

Johnny didn't move. It was as though he'd been sewn into the threadbare cot he slept on.

When he didn't stand like ordered, the sergeant grabbed him under the arms and hoisted him up. "It's time to go."

Johnny didn't struggle against the bigger man. What was the point? He'd learned that lesson during his time in captivity while being ridiculed, stripped, and paraded from one Rebel camp to another.

"We've had our fill of the Yankee fighting baby," the lieutenant told him. "You've been paroled."

Johnny jerked to a halt, turned and stared at the lieutenant. "Paroled? Does that mean I'm going home?" he dared to ask.

"It does. You've been exchanged and will be returned to Columbus, Ohio, to rejoin your regiment."

Too stunned, Johnny said nothing. All he could think about were his weeks of captivity. He'd been starved, kept alive at the whim of a few men. He'd no longer be taunted then thrown into a tiny, dirty cell or room with no sunlight and only the bugs and rats to keep him company.

He was going home.

Stopped in Cincinnati on his way to rejoin the regiment, Johnny learned that General Rosecrans had a residence there. He recalled their meeting at Chickamauga. When Rosecrans told him that if he ever found himself in the same location, Johnny should seek him out.

Two hours later, Johnny was sitting on a sofa in the Burnett House, the General's current residence.

"May I bring you some milk and cookies young man?" Mrs. Saunders, the proprietor's wife, asked.

Johnny was annoyed he'd been offered milk and cookies. If another soldier were sitting in this very spot, would she have offered *him* the same? Despite his irritation, the refreshments sounded wonderful. He jerked his hat off and managed a strangled, "Yes, Ma'am. Thank you, Ma'am."

"Very well, I shall return shortly." Johnny waited on the sofa. His feet dangled over the edge when he sat back.

A few minutes later, Mrs. Saunders returned. Johnny couldn't remember the last time he'd had such a delicious treat, but forced himself to eat slowly and with dignity.

Before Mrs. Saunders left the room, she smiled. "It's good to see a growing boy eat. I shall let the General know you are here as soon as he arrives."

Johnny cringed at her reference. He'd done everything in his power to be looked upon as a soldier, not a boy. It seemed he still had far to go.

General Rosecrans arrived a half hour later. Johnny scooted to the edge of the sofa, jumped to his feet and saluted. "Sir!"

The General returned the salute. "I fear I'm at a disadvantage. Who might you be, young man?"

Johnny's chin came up. "I am Johnny Clem. Drummer boy from Company C of the 22nd Michigan Volunteer Infantry, Sir. We spoke at Chickamauga."

"Ah, yes, now I recall. Welcome, Johnny Clem, drummer boy of Company C."

"You told me to come see you, Sir, if we were ever in the same place."

"Indeed, I did. And here you are." There was a trace of humor in his voice and his eyes twinkled. "I'm glad you survived the battle, Johnny Clem."

"Me too," he said with great enthusiasm. "I was captured a few weeks later, though, and spent a couple of months with those dirty...sorry, Sir, with the Rebels."

"I'd like to hear about it." Rosecrans waved for Johnny to return to his seat on the sofa. The General sat down in a wing-back chair nearby and crossed his legs. He folded his hands, assuming the posture of someone who had an interest in what Johnny had to say.

Johnny regaled the General with his tale of how he'd played dead at Chickamauga and had shot the Confederate Colonel. His time at Moccasin Point and, finally, his capture while on provost duty with the supply train.

Rosecrans studied Johnny a moment then said, "You are quite a remarkable young man."

"Thank you, Sir." Pride washed over Johnny.

The General stood. "Will you excuse me a moment?"

Johnny jumped to his feet. "Of course, Sir."

When the General returned a few minutes later, he stepped in front of Johnny. Mrs. Saunders followed the General into the room, a huge grin on her face.

"Johnny Clem, yours is a story of perseverance and courage, one that should be known by many a man. And boy." He turned to Mrs. Saunders, who handed him a square piece of cloth. "Because of your bravery and ill-treatment while in captivity," he said when he turned back, "I bestow upon you the Army of the Cumberland's 'Roll of Honor.'"

The General lifted the patch in front of Johnny. General Rosecrans's face was displayed at the center of the award. Johnny's full name, age, regiment, and other pertinent information had been filled in. His mouth gaped open. Words wouldn't form in his brain, let alone come out. He knew the honor he was being given wasn't granted easily or to many men. Only those who showed praiseworthy actions on the battlefield received it.

Mrs. Saunders stepped beside him. "If you give me a few minutes, I shall sew this onto your frock before you leave." She helped Johnny slip off his coat and exited the room with it draped across her arm.

Mrs. Saunders returned shortly with the award affixed to his coat.

Johnny stared down at the patch. He ran his fingers over the cloth. He'd thought he couldn't get a better gift than what Harve, Company C, and General Thomas had given to him. This honor was beyond anything he'd ever dreamed.

"Let me help you with that." Rosecrans took Johnny's frock and helped him slide it on.

Mrs. Saunders smoothed the material over his shoulders and picked off invisible lint. She stepped back, her eyes aglow. "That is one handsome...soldier, General Rosecrans."

"Indeed, he is, Mrs. Saunders. Indeed, he is. One I am proud to have among my ranks." He snapped a brisk salute.

Johnny returned the action, his frame straight. Pride coursed through him.

Johnny had to know what had become of Harve. At each stop on his way to Columbus, he checked the boards of the dead and wounded. He'd learned that Harve and most of the men captured from the 22nd had been sent to Andersonville. Following his own capture, Johnny had had nightmares about winding up there too. The only good thought about that was that he would be with Harve. Everything else about the place terrified him.

In Cincinnati, following his meeting with General Rosecrans, he found his way to the town square.

After asking several citizens where he could find the postings, he stood in front of a large wooden board that displayed various battles, those who had been wounded, captured and killed.

He scoured the listing for what was becoming known as the Battle at Chickamauga, named for the creek nearby. He found the 22nd Michigan and the names of so many of his comrades who were listed as dead or captured. Colonel LeFavour now resided at Libby. He searched for Harve's name and found it.

His eyes blurred. He tried to hold back the tears, but failed. His friend was listed as deceased.

Johnny recalled the wound Harve had gotten in battle. The one he'd told Johnny was nothing but a scratch. Without proper medical attention, it must have festered and...

Johnny sat down on a nearby bench, took off his hat, and said a prayer like he'd heard Preacher Harris do many times before he'd left Newark. Although sadness nearly consumed Johnny, at least he finally knew what had become of his friend.

When Johnny returned to the 22nd Michigan, a very important-looking letter awaited him. One with a military seal and Major General Thomas's name on it.

He sat down, opened it, and read it twice to understand what it said.

"Sergeant John Lincoln Clem is hereby ordered to report as a mounted orderly in the service of Major General Thomas. This order is effective immediately."

It took a few moments to sink in before Johnny understood he was no longer just a drummer boy or even a sergeant of Company C. He was a soldier, a real soldier, assigned to a major general. Yet another honor few men achieved in their military career, no matter what their age.

Johnny jumped to his feet, threw his few belongings into his haversack, and headed for command, prepared to do his duty.

Johnny was eight months shy of turning thirteen.

"Little" Johnny Clem
Drummer Boy of Chickamauga

Sergeant John "Johnny" Clem

Afterword

Once again, history is a winding, overgrown, twisting path not easy to follow. It is filled with conflicting reports.

According to accounts about his life, John "Johnny" Clem said that after his mother's death, he tried to join up with the 3rd Ohio Infantry regiment but was turned away because of his age. He states he was nine or ten when this happened. I found information stating that he drilled with the 3rd while they were in Newark, so it stands to reason if he intended to enlist following his mother's death, he would have tried to do so with them first. Most likely, he tried and was turned away. Who can say for certain what happened before he began to follow the 22nd?

However, the *Licking County Library's Wiki!* (see references) states: "Clem hopped aboard a train that was transporting the regiment [the 3rd Ohio]. He stayed hidden aboard a baggage car until he arrived with the regiment at its destination of Camp Dennison in Cincinnati, Ohio. Clem's father, Roman, went to Cincinnati to retrieve his son, but Johnny was able to evade him." In this version it says the men of the 3rd gave him food and wages and the role of drummer boy—not the 22nd.

He is also credited with participating in the Battle of Shiloh (April 6-7, 1862) and "demonstrated his calmness under fire" when a Confederate cannonball supposedly smashed his drum while he was playing it. *Could* he have been with the 3rd at Shiloh, then left that regiment to join the 22nd Michigan, which began recruiting three months later, in July of '62? Or was his being with the 3rd a fabrication on his part as some historians believe?

"Some scholars now contend that Union reporters enhanced Clem's exploits to help promote the war effort." (*Ohio History Central*-see references.) However, his joining the 22nd Michigan when he was eleven has been documented.

Harve is a figment of my imagination.

At the Battle of Chickamauga, some accounts say Johnny "rode a caisson into battle." Some say he killed the Confederate Colonel he shot.

At Chickamauga, the 22nd Michigan Volunteer Infantry suffered huge losses. They were believed to be the last regiment that left Horseshoe Ridge due to a lack of communication. Of the 455 men in that regiment who fought on the ridge, 32 were killed. 96 were wounded and 261 were taken as prisoners of war for a casualty rate of 85%. Colonel LeFavour was captured and survived prison, but was killed when thrown from his carriage in 1878 in Pawtucket, Rhode Island. He was forty years old.

Of the 997 men who left Pontiac the previous September, only 187 men remained. 178 men, including 14 officers, were taken prisoner and sent to Libby, Danville, or Andersonville prisons, never to return home. In notice of their bravery following the Battle of Chickamauga, the 22nd received engineering and provost duties.

Some accounts have General Thomas giving Johnny his promotion, others give that distinction to General Rosecrans. Some accounts have Johnny in captivity for only three days before he was paroled. Others have him in captivity for over sixty days before he was sent to Camp Chase in Ohio to await exchange. In that time, he was paraded around as a poster boy by the Confederates for the Union's recruitment of "babies" into service. Even the newspapers of the time carry conflicting stories.

The 22nd Michigan was mustered out of service on June 26, 1865 in Nashville, Tennessee.

After the war, Johnny returned to Newark and graduated from Newark High School in 1870. He rejoined the army in 1871 as a second lieutenant. He married Anita French in 1875 and had six children. Sadly, five of those children died before reaching adulthood. John L. (Lincoln) Clem remained in the military for forty-five years before retiring as a Brigadier General. Clem died on May 13, 1937 at his home in San Antonio, Texas. He is buried in Arlington National Cemetery in Washington, D.C.

Numerous discrepancies describe the early life of John, Johnny, Clem, "The Little Drummer Boy of Chickamauga." Those discrepancies may never be proven one way or another.

Resources

Ohio History Central:
https://ohiohistorycentral.org/w/Johnny_Klem

Licking County Library:
http://wiki.lickingcountylibrary.info/Johnny_Clem

22nd Regiment Michigan Infantry:
www.migenweb.org/michiganinthewar/infantry/22
ndinf.htm

*American Civil War Research Database
Regiment History: Michigan Twenty-Second
Infantry (Three Years)*
http://www.civilwardata.com/active/hdsquery.dll?
RegimentHistory?1099&U

Ancestral Findings:
https://ancestralfindings.com/john-clem-the-
unsung-heroes-of-the-civil-war/

The Washington Post:
https://www.washingtonpost.com/lifestyle/kidspos
t/drummer-boys-played-important-roles-in-the-civil-war-
and-some-became-
soldiers/2012/01/31/gIQA3cKzRR_story.html

*National Park Service: Civil War: Battle Unit
Details/Union Michigan Volunteers/22nd Regiment,
Michigan Infantry*
https://www.nps.gov/civilwar/search-battle-units-
detail.htm?battleUnitCode=UMI0022RI

*The Gallant Stand of the 22nd Michigan,
September 20, 1863*:
https://www.westerntheatercivilwar.com/post/the-gallant-stand-of-the-22nd-michigan-september-20-1863

Wikipedia:
https://en.wikipedia.org/wiki/John_Clem#:~:text=Arlington%20National%20Cemetery.-,Dates%20of%20promotion,1863%20to%2019%20September%201864

*Newark Advocate/Veterans Column: Johnny Clem
is captured by Confederates:*
https://www.newarkadvocate.com/story/news/local/2019/01/11/veterans-column-johnny-clem-captured-confederates/2523866002/ (cited) *Too Young to Die, Boy Soldiers of the Union Army,* by Dennis Keesee, Blue Acorn Press, 2001

YesterYear Once More – Johnny Clem: The Boy of Chickamauga:
https://yesteryearsnews.wordpress.com/2009/11/06/johnny-clem-the-boy-of-chickamauga/ (From *The Daily Gazette* (Janesville, Wisconsin) Dec 18, 1863)

Shoot Out at Roscoe

March 16, 1874

John Younger took a long pull on his cigar. He lowered his hand to rest on the arm of the overstuffed chair he sat in, careful not to dislodge the growing ash. Eyes hooded, he studied the brightly lit main salon of the Monegaw Hotel, built on a hilltop near Monegaw Creek and overlooking the Osage River and sulfur springs below. John was at ease here. Thanks to his older brother, Cole, he knew the surrounding area well. Cole had spent much of his youth exploring the nearby region where their grandfather Charles once owned a 240-acre spread. That was until '61 when the hotel and the town of Osceola, Missouri, were both burned by Kansan James Lane at the start of the War of Northern Aggression.

Then everything changed.

Rebuilt as a resort after the war, the hotel now boasted a lively clientele who enjoyed the medicinal properties of the sulfur springs. People came from miles around to enjoy the proclaimed healing waters. The guests spent hours in the baths or lounging in the salon with Jules Verne's recently released *Journey to the Center of the Earth* or well-established tomes like Alexander Dumas's *The Count of Monte Cristo* and *The Three Musketeers*

John snickered. The resort was easy to find. Just follow the stench of rotten eggs that came from the springs. On more than one occasion when on the run, he and his brothers had easily located the cave hidden above the hotel by following the acrid odors below.

Now John and his brothers, Cole the oldest at thirty, Jim at twenty-six, John in the middle at twenty-three, and Bob, the youngest at twenty-one, came often to the resort to enjoy both its healing and social amenities.

Tonight, only John and Jim were here. John stared across the room at his brother, dancing with a pretty blonde. Laughing as though he had not a care in the world. *He* was having a good time. John was not, as so often happened whenever he reflected on his life.

Perhaps there was nothing to worry about right this moment, but who knew what tomorrow would bring, considering the way they lived their lives? Running and hiding from the law. Sometimes he wished it could be different, but nothing could change the past and he accepted that.

He let his head rest against the back of the chair, wishing he could stay here and forget the often-brutal twists and turns his life had taken since the war ended. But he and Jim had business with Cole in Arkansas.

John's thoughts turned to his father as they often did when he contemplated his life and where it had brought him. His gut clenched. Eighty miles might separate Harrisonville from Monegaw Springs, but it wasn't far enough to forget his father's murder twelve years ago—and everything that came after.

John frowned and shook his head. Maybe it was time for him to leave before his mood soured further.

He took another draw on his cigar and considered the salon. Tonight's dance reminded John of many nights he'd spent here. Well-dressed men and women milled around the room lined with plush, colorful settees and overstuffed chairs. The patrons gathered in small clusters to chat, drink, and socialize. Others danced to lively music played by a small string band. It was raucous and loud. The way John liked it. Here, he blended in. He wasn't one of the hated Younger boys. He was just John.

A pretty brunette stepped beside him and placed her hand on his shoulder. She leaned toward him, exposing a broad hint of cleavage, and pushed a lock of John's always unruly hair off his forehead. "You look like a man who needs some cheering up. Perhaps a dance might help?" Her smile was wide, her deep green eyes probing.

John was irritated, but not by Althea's interruption. It was his dark thoughts of what the Federals had done to his family, to his father, Cole, even to his mother and sister, harassing them like criminals, that always fueled a fury in him. Today was no different. His near lifetime of rage had descended upon him in a heartbeat.

He took a deep, calming breath, turned, and smiled at the petite woman beside him, her eyes glowing in the light from the chandelier above. Althea was a regular at the dances. He'd gotten to know her in recent years. She knew who he was. Knew what had happened to his father, to him during the war, and after, and she sympathized. She accepted him for who he was and had told him on many occasions she was happy to enjoy his company whenever she could. Her companionship was always welcomed.

John pushed his weighty thoughts into the recesses of his mind. He kissed Althea on the cheek. "I'd love to dance, darlin'." He put his cigar in the tray beside the chair and got to his feet. He took her hand and twirled her in several circles before pulling her to his chest. He danced away his anger, saving it for another time when he could do something about it.

Jim Younger grunted and shaded his eyes from the bright sunlight streaking in through the window. He lifted his hands to stop the onslaught of someone slapping his face. If they didn't stop soon, there was going to be hell to pay.

He flailed his arms to knock away his abuser. "Enough!" When he opened his eyes, his brother stood leering at him.

John stepped back. "About time. I thought you were going to sleep the day away."

Fully awake now, Jim jerked upright, but fell back when lights exploded behind his eyes. He groaned and grabbed his head. "Damn. Guess I had too much fun last night."

"We both did, but it's time to git around. Cole's waiting," John reminded him.

Jim glowered in response. "Dang it, John, Cole's in Hot Springs. Not down the road or even in the next county. Why are you in such an all-fired hurry to get there?" He rubbed his temple to stop the throbbing.

"We told him we'd be there by the end of the week. It's time to git going."

Jim pushed himself upright. When the room stopped spinning, he swung his legs to the floor. Once steady, he stood, grabbed his hat from the peg beside the bed, and started for the door, groaning against the pain in his head.

John followed. "The horses are saddled and ready to go. Wouldn't want you to over-tax yourself too much, big brother," he goaded.

Several miles down the road, Jim's stomach started to grumble. "You hungry?" he asked John. "I'm starved. Let's ride by Theo's place and get some grub." Jim turned his mount toward Theo Snuffer's place, the man who had convinced his grandfather Charles to move to the area in 1850 in what started an avalanche of irreversible events for the Younger family.

"I'm right behind you. I'm so hungry I could eat a full stack of Ma's flapjacks without takin' a breath," John said.

Sadness washed over Jim. He missed his deceased mother more than he liked to admit, but he refused to dwell on it. It only ruined his mood, which was already sour.

On the outskirts of Roscoe, he and John turned their mounts up the Chalk Level Road and rode in companionable silence toward the home of their old family friend.

"Jim! John! Come on in you two young reprobates." Theo, stooped by time, swung the door wide and moved aside for the boys to enter.

The brothers stomped the dust off their boots, slapped their hats across their legs, then stepped inside.

"To what do I owe this pleasure?" Theo asked.

"We're headed to meet Cole in Arkansas," Jim told Theo. "Didn't git a chance to eat this mornin' and I'm as hungry as a bear."

"You came to the right place. Set down and I'll git you some food. You know I'll do whatever I can for Charlie's kin." He hurried away as fast as his aged legs allowed.

Jim, his stomach growling, plopped down on the bench. He placed his elbows on the table and settled his chin in his hands. The glint of the sun hit him in the face, so he closed his eyes against the pain it caused in his head. In moments, he was asleep.

Charlie's kin. John frowned at Theo's reference. He and his siblings were Charlie's *legitimate* grandchildren. The ones he *hadn't* bequeathed his Osceola acreage to. Instead, he'd given it all to Elizabeth, the mulatto woman he'd openly lived with for the four years he'd resided there, along with her children, Catherine and Simpson, whom he legitimized upon his death by giving them their freedom—and his name.

Thoughts of his grandfather triggered an array of memories John didn't want to recall. He tried to ignore them, but they crowded his mind anyway. The old man had been gone for twenty years, since '54, but what he'd done to the family still angered John. He may have been a toddler when the old man died, but tales of what he'd done had filled more than one family conversation through the years.

He shook his head to stop the unwanted thoughts. Who was he to judge? His own indiscretions crashed down on him. He'd done much he wasn't proud of in his short life. But he'd had no choice. He'd been too young to join up with Quantrill in the early years of the war like Cole and Jim had done after their father was murdered on his way home from a business trip in July of '62.

Everyone knew who had killed Henry Younger, a former mayor of Harrisonville. It was that damned Lieutenant Irvin Walley who, when Cole was seventeen years old, had decided Cole was a spy and promised to hunt him down and hang him. The threat had sent Cole into hiding first, then into the arms of William Clarke Quantrill and his Bushwhackers. When Walley couldn't catch Cole, he'd settled for his father. Found with three thousand dollars on his person, it wasn't a robbery, so what other motive would explain Henry Younger's murder? No one would say, officially. The Federals certainly hadn't. It wouldn't do for them to condemn one of their own.

Although he and Bob, only twelve and ten at the time of his father's murder, couldn't join up with Cole and Jim, it didn't mean the war hadn't touched them.

John closed his eyes against the visage that swooped into his mind of the first man he'd shot and killed. Shortly after the end of the war, a former Federal had recognized John as kin to Cole. His brother's brutal legacy of riding with Quantrill's Raiders during the war harbored much ill will by some of the locals.

The soldier had trotted his horse alongside their wagon and verbally accosted his family with disparaging comments about Cole, causing his mother and sister great distress.

John had tried to get the man to stop his attack, but the former soldier had been set on humiliating him, a mere fifteen-years-old at the time.

John grunted and touched the spot on his face where a frozen fish, wielded by the angry soldier, had struck him more than once. He sighed, recalling how he'd begged the man to stop. When the soldier refused, John had stood, opened the wagon box, and pulled a recently repaired pistol of Cole's from inside. Without further hesitation, he shot the man between the eyes.

John was immediately picked up by the authorities, the man's body taken away. When examined, a weighted slingshot was found tied to his wrist. A weapon to be sure. John was released as having acted in self-defense.

His mother, Bersheba, in an attempt to escape the persecution that followed her family, had fled with her children to Texas. She wanted only to be left alone.

It wasn't to be.

The Youngers had been in Texas for four years when Bersheba became ill. She'd told her sons she was tired of running. She'd lived her whole life in Missouri and intended to die there. John had been at her bedside when she instructed her children to, "Take me home."

John scrubbed at his face. If only they *had* been left alone when they got back to Missouri, things might be different. So different.

His legs grew unsteady with the barrage of memories. John strode around the table and dropped onto the bench seat opposite Jim. He tried to dispel the thoughts that pummeled him, but they filled every corner of his mind.

He glanced at his brother, who had his chin cradled in his hands, his lips puffing out with each exhaled breath. John shook his head. If only he could put his mind to rest that easily.

While he waited for Theo, John's thoughts returned to his difficult past. He fingered the thick scar on his neck. His nostrils flared and he ground his teeth with the rage that filled him. They hadn't been back in Missouri long before a posse descended upon their home, seeking information about Cole.

In their frustration, when none of the Youngers would divulge Cole's whereabouts, Bob was knocked unconscious. John was dragged out back—and hanged. Four times they stretched his neck, lifting him off the ground kicking and thrashing, gagging for breath. When he was dropped to his feet the last time, he was helpless to stop them when they fell upon him with knives, cutting and slicing until he was left bloody and near death.

He could still see his mother on her knees. Hear her piteous wails begging them to stop.

John jerked his fingers away from the scar as though burned. He blinked furiously. Heart racing, he sucked in a deep breath to calm himself. The familiar fury was building again. Although he'd survived the hanging and brutal knife attack, his mother had not. The horror of it had sent her to her grave. And the brothers into a tailspin.

175

John and Bob had buried their mother, then joined up with Jim, already gone from home. John grimaced at how their lives changed after that, traveling between Texas and Missouri. John's path of lawlessness had been set there after he killed two Texas Deputy Sheriffs in a shootout when they'd tried to arrest him. Then a year ago, in 1873, John, Bob, and Jim joined up with big brother Cole. An outlaw.

John shoved his hands through his hair and tried to suppress the brutal images in his head, but they battered him without cease until Theo returned with a tray of food.

"Git it while it's hot, boys," the older man crooned.

Jim's head snapped up and he immediately began scooping up spoonsful of eggs and bacon.

Although John's stomach bucked with hunger, he couldn't dispel the visions in his mind. He didn't speak as he filled his plate and opened his mouth only to eat.

The three men were halfway through their meal when their chins snapped up in unison.

"Horses coming," Theo said. "Git on up to the loft."

"You don't have to tell us twice." John grabbed his pistol from beside his plate where he'd set it. Jim did the same. Both scurried up the steps and fell against the wall. Gaps in the wooden slats allowed them to see and hear the men below.

Theo stomped onto the porch, snapping his suspenders into place over his belly and chest. He greeted the two men on horseback. "Good mornin', gents. I'm Theo Snuffer. Can I help you with somethin'?"

One man nudged his mount forward. "I am Mr. Allen." He turned to his companion who hung back, his face hidden beneath his hat. "This is Mr. Daniels. We're cattle buyers searching for the home of the widow Simms who has some cattle for sale."

"Sure, the widow Simms." Theo pointed in the direction of the Simms place. "She lives thata way. Straight out. You can't miss it."

"Thank you for your time." Allen tipped his hat. The two men spun their mounts around and started away.

Theo put one foot inside the door but stopped and turned to watch the departing men. He scratched his head.

The old man watched them ride for a few minutes, then hurried inside. "Come on down, boys."

Jim went back to eating as though nothing had happened. Between mouthfuls he said to John, stomping back and forth behind him, "They're cattle buyers. Relax, will ya?"

"If they're cattle buyers looking for the widow Simms, why are they going in the opposite direction Theo told them to go?" John asked from where he stood in front of the window. "They're Pinkertons, I tell you. I know they are. They're sniffing around to see if they can find us. I'd bet my share of our next job on it."

"You might be right," Theo said, picking his teeth. "They was awful well-armed to be cattle buyers. That other one hung back, so I couldn't see his face. He stayed quiet. Was nervous, too. Acted like he was hidin' somethin'."

Jim pushed his plate away. He stood and stepped over the bench seat. "So, what are we supposed to do?" He cocked his head at John.

John hesitated a moment before his lips curled into a smile. "We go after 'em and find out who they are."

Jim held up his hands, palms out. "Now hold on, little brother. There's no reason to go off looking for trouble. We should mind our business and let 'em be. And they'll let us be."

177

John shook his head and sniggered. "I don't see anybody letting the Youngers be. Especially not Pinkerton Detectives. I say we go after 'em." John glared at Jim. "If you don't go with me, I'll go by myself."

Jim groaned. "You know I'm not gonna let you go after trouble alone." He grabbed his hat and shoved it on his head. "Thanks for breakfast, Theo." He started for the back door where the horses were hidden, then jerked to a halt. He looked over his shoulder and snapped at John, "You coming?"

John mounted his horse, Jim beside him, and headed after the supposed cattle buyers. Jim carried a pistol on each hip. John had a pistol on his right hip and his double-barrel shotgun in his right hand.

They'd gone barely a quarter of a mile when John spotted the men walking their horses up the road. He pointed. "There they are."

"And someone else is with 'em," Jim said.

They heeled their horses into a trot.

The suspected Pinkertons turned around when they heard the approaching riders.

"They're Pinkertons all right," John said. "I got no doubt. Why else would they meet another man out here on the road?" He leveled his shotgun and sent his horse into a lope.

The man who had joined Allen and Daniels stared a few moments as John and Jim approached. Then he sent his horse galloping into the open field that ran along the road and into a copse of trees.

Using his knees to guide his horse, Jim slid his pistols from their holsters and fired. One shot sent the fleeing man's hat into the air. He seemed not to notice, kicking his horse in a wild frenzy until they disappeared into the trees.

"Let's git the other two," John shouted, cantering his horse beside Jim's. He leveled his shotgun at the man who had called himself Mr. Allen.

"Right beside you," Jim responded, his pistols aimed ahead.

They reined their horses to a jarring halt in front of the alleged Pinkertons.

"Drop your guns and put up your hands. Both of you." John wagged his shotgun at them.

The men threw down their weapons and put their hands up.

Jim slipped one of his pistols back into its holster, dismounted and gathered up the discarded guns. "What have we here?" He eyed a Trantor .43 caliber rifle. "That's one nice piece of English weaponry." He lifted it for John to see then waved it at Allen. "Thanks for the present. I'll be sure to enjoy it." He winked at the gun's former owner.

"You told Snuffer you were cattle buyers. Who are you? Really?" John's tone was hard.

"We told you," the one who had introduced himself as Allen said. "We are cattle buyers. From Osceola."

"What the hell are you doing in Roscoe then? That isn't but the next town over," Jim asked.

"We're just wandering around. No harm in that, is there?" Allen said as though it was the most natural thing for him and his companion to roam the countryside for no reason.

John pursed his lips. He leaned forward in the saddle, placed his arms across the horn and said, "Admit you're Pinkertons."

"No, sir, we're not," Allen said with a vehement shake of his head. "We're cattle buyers."

"Then why are you so heavily armed?" Jim asked.

"We have a right to be armed. To protect ourselves," Allen protested. His gloved fingers thrummed his leg.

John swung his shotgun at the man who remained silent on his mount. "You got anything to say, mister?"

The brim of his hat obscured his face, but he gave a quick shake of his head.

John's attention was drawn by movement to his left. Allen was pointing a small caliber pistol straight at him. John rotated and cocked his shotgun at the same time. He leveled it at Allen and pulled the triggers. The full force of both barrels rained down on the man. He shrieked when buckshot peppered him in the arm and shoulder.

But Allen had gotten a shot off too.

John was thrown back in the saddle when a bullet struck him in the throat. He clutched his neck with one hand and grabbed the horn with his other to keep from falling off his horse.

Jim screamed his name.

John was trying not to panic, when Jim's pistol exploded beside him.

With all the strength he could muster, John pulled himself upright, withdrew his kerchief from his vest pocket, and wrapped it around his neck. He noted with confusion that Allen was still in the saddle and quite alive. Somehow, Jim had missed the man when he shot at him.

Jim lifted his pistol to fire at Allen a second time, but Allen's hands were empty, his gun in the dirt. The two men stared at each other for several heartbeats before Allen wheeled his horse around and kicked it into a gallop toward the field.

The quiet man swung his mount to follow Allen.

180

"No you don't," Jim ground out. He took a moment to steady himself, aimed, and fired. The second fleeing man clawed at his neck, swayed in the saddle, then toppled to the ground.

John was angry. No, he was furious that the Pinkerton man had gotten the drop on him. He sent his horse into a gallop after his prey.

The Pinkerton man made it to the woods.

John wasn't far behind when Allen ran smack into a low-hanging tree limb. He tumbled from his saddle into a thicket of bushes.

John reined up close to where Allen had fallen. He spotted him lying on his back in the bushes. The man's eyes went wide when he saw John sitting his horse above him. John merely shook his head, took aim, and fired. A bright red patch of blood spread across his chest.

When John spun his horse around, the movement made him light-headed. He slowed the animal and took his time heading back to Jim, waiting for him beyond the McFerrin's hog pen up the road. He didn't need to rush. The danger was over. He had plenty of time.

He was halfway across the field when his throat began to ache. He touched the neckerchief where the bullet had struck him. When he pulled his fingers away, they were covered with blood. Bile filled his mouth. He couldn't feel his hands. He was cold, so cold. He gripped the horn with both hands to keep from swaying in the saddle. The sun seemed to be disappearing in front of his eyes.

He had to reach Jim. Everything would be all right when he got to Jim. As he drew closer, his brother's visage became fuzzy in the dimming light. John tried to call Jim's name, but nothing came out.

He barely made out Jim running toward him.

"John!" his brother screamed.

Before Jim reached him, the pain ceased and the light disappeared.

*

Jim ran to his fallen brother. "No, no, no, no no!" he cried, his boots hitting the ground as quickly as he could make them go. When he reached John, he dropped to his knees beside him, hauled his brother into his arms, and pulled him to his chest. He rocked back and forth, talking softly. "I'll get you out of here, John. We'll get on our way to Arkansas and hook up with Cole and Bob. You'll see. You're gonna be fine."

Although bereft and in denial that his brother was dead, he wasn't unaware of his surroundings. He whipped out his gun and whirled when someone came up on him.

"Dang it, Speed, I almost shot you and Ol," he said to the two farmers who lived nearby, George "Speed" McDonald and Ol Davis.

"We seen it all," Speed told Jim. "What kin we do?"

Jim smoothed the always errant wave of hair from John's forehead. His face was as pale as a bedsheet, the kerchief around his neck soaked with blood. Jim couldn't deny it. John was dead. "I guess this is it, little brother. I'll see you on the other side." He closed John's eyes and laid him in the grass. With a last look, he removed John's personal items, then handed Speed John's pistol. "Watch over him till Theo gets here. I'm headed to his place now."

"I'll do it, Jim. I'm powerful sorry John's..."

Jim swallowed and laid his hand on the farmer's shoulder. "I know, Speed. Thanks for the help. Make sure nobody gets to his body. More'n one local might like to set his head on a pike or hang his body out for the crows to pick at his eyes."

"It's a fact. Folks don't cotton to, to—"

"Outlaws," Jim finished for him.

The man shoved his hands into his pockets, lowered his eyes, and nodded.

"I'm sorry too," Ol Davis told Jim.

"Thanks boys." He mounted and sent his horse into a gallop the short distance to Theo Snuffer's place.

When Jim arrived a few minutes later, he was off the horse before it came to a full stop. "Theo! Theo!" He nearly knocked the old man down as he hurried from the house to greet Jim.

"What is it?" Theo looked around, alarm in his eyes.

Jim grabbed the older man by his upper arms. "John's dead. Shot by Pinkertons."

"Them boys that was here earlier?"

Jim nodded. "We caught up to them not far from here where they joined up with another man. He didn't stick around long, though. Hightailed it as soon as he spotted me and John. The one that called himself Mr. Allen and the other one, Daniels, are both dead." He scrubbed at his face then added, "I shot the one who never said a word. John chased Allen into the trees and shot him, but not before John took a bullet in his neck."

"What do you want me to do?" Theo asked.

"Go get him. He's over in the hog pen near the McFerrin place. Speed McDonald is watching over him. Don't want anybody to desecrate his...body before you get there," he said, a hitch in his voice.

"I'll git over there right now." Theo hugged him. "I'm so sorry, Jim. So sorry. I'll take care of him."

"I know you will."

"What're you gonna do?" Theo asked when he stepped back.

Jim shook his head. He hadn't thought much farther than getting John's body taken care of. He knew, for certain, it wouldn't take long for a posse to form and come after him. Two Pinkerton men were dead, after all, by his and John's hands.

He sighed and shrugged. "Guess all I can do is slap leather outta here. Won't be long before a posse gathers. I plan to be long gone before they do. I'll head for Arkansas to meet Cole and Bob."

Theo nodded agreement. "You watch out fer yourself. We don't want to lose no other brothers."

Jim nodded again. "Thanks for being such a good friend, Theo." He forced his feet to move and went to his horse. He mounted and rode away, wishing the pain that filled his soul could be left behind as easily as Theo—and his brother.

Afterword

When Snuffer reached John's body, a crowd had gathered, the folks in town having heard the gunshots. Mr. Allen, in reality Captain Louis Lull of the Pinkerton Detective Agency, had also been found. Alive.

John's body was moved to the nearby McFerrin home and left under heavy guard to keep his corpse from being desecrated by angry townspeople over the death of the "quiet man," local Deputy Sheriff Edwin Daniels who had acted as a guide for the Pinkertons and was well-loved by the locals.

Later that day, Daniels's body and Lull were removed to the Roscoe Hotel.

The following morning, March 18th, Snuffer returned to the McFerrin home, claimed John's body, and took him back to his place. He buried him under a large cedar tree on his property. John's body was later removed and interred at the Yeater Cemetery in Roscoe where it rests today.

Louis Lull, the Pinkerton detective, was given medical attention in Roscoe. When his wife and William Pinkerton arrived, he was transferred to Osceola where a prominent Civil War surgeon tended him until his death shortly thereafter.

The unknown man who met Lull and Daniels was John Boyle, another Pinkerton detective who used the alias of James Wright.

In 1876, after the botched bank robbery in Northfield, Minnesota by the James/Younger Gang and the long chase that followed, Cole, Jim and Bob Younger were finally captured.

Cole sustained injuries to his jaw, four bullet wounds in the back, buckshot in his left shoulder, another in his arm, and another behind his armpit.

Jim's injuries included a ball in his upper jaw that destroyed his jawbone. He was also hit by buckshot in his middle thigh.

Bob's wounds included a ball that entered his shoulder blade and exited through his chest. He sustained a broken arm in Northfield, which was nearly healed by the time they were caught and he was examined by a doctor.

Cole, Jim, and Bob pled guilty to their crimes to keep from being hanged. All three were sentenced to life in prison at the Minnesota Territorial Prison in Stillwater.

Bob died there in 1889.

Thanks to supporters who lobbied for Cole and Jim's release, they were both paroled on July 1, 1901.

Cole lived to be seventy-two years old. He died on March 21, 1916, and is buried in Lee's Summit, Missouri.

Jim committed suicide on October 19, 1902, a year after his release from prison. He was fifty-four. He had been in a romantic relationship with Alix Muller, whom he'd met twenty years after the Northfield robbery while he was still in prison. The two were engaged to be married. However, due to the terms of his parole, he wasn't allowed to marry and committed suicide instead.

Resources

John Younger (1851-March 17, 1874), American Outlaw / World Biographical Encyclopedia:
https://prabook.com/web/john.younger/2228026

A Little History of Monegaw Springs:
http://www.tipcoleman.com/#:~:text=Monegaw%20Sprin gs%20was%20one%20of,Lane%20and%20his%20Kansa s%20Jayhawkers.

Oklahoma Historical Society:
https://www.okhistory.org/publications/enc/entry. php?entry=YO003

The Roscoe Gunfight: The Youngers vs. The Pinkertons:
https://www.angelfire.com/mi2/jamesyoungergang /roscoe.html

Wiki Tree: Charles Lee Younger:
https://www.wikitree.com/wiki/Younger-266

Special thanks to Rob Heckenlively and his wife Teresa, owners of the Old/Historic Commercial Hotel in Osceola, Missouri. Teresa's tour of the hotel (including the Jesse James room and other interesting historic facts) and Rob's tour of Osceola and his great commentary on what happened the day John Younger was killed in Roscoe, is what piqued my interest to write this story.

SNIPPETS-Book Two   *D.L. Rogers*

Maria Isabella (Belle) Boyd
The "Cleopatra of Secession"

May 5, 1861

"When shall I see you again?" Tears filled the eyes of seventeen-year-old Maria Isabella Boyd, better known as Belle. She stepped closer to her father, standing in the entryway of their home. Her mother, Mary, stood behind them, awaiting her turn to bid her husband goodbye.

Benjamin Boyd gathered his daughter into his arms and held her tight. When the embrace ended, she stepped back and swiped the offensive tears from her cheeks. Belle Boyd cried only to get her way, not when she sent her father off to war.

Belle reached for his hands. "I know why you're going. You must do your duty for the Cause. I fully support your decision."

Her father, a prosperous shopkeeper in the town of Martinsburg, Virginia, was leaving for Harper's Ferry, twenty miles away. There, he intended to join up with Colonel Thomas J. Jackson's Confederate 2nd Virginia command.

What northerners called the War of the Rebellion and southerners called the War of Northern Aggression, had been brewing for a long time. The nation had been on the cusp of an all-out conflict since before secession fever gripped the country last year. When South Carolina seceded in December of 1860, Mississippi, Florida, Alabama, Georgia, Louisiana, Texas, then Virginia, had followed. The seceding states wanted to be left alone to govern themselves without interference by the Federal

Government. Most of their residents held slaves, even Robert E. Lee, a former West Pointer, who had been approached to lead the Union army. But he'd sided with his home state and the Confederacy, citing his inability to make war against his beloved Virginia.

However, the majority of citizens of Martinsburg, in the northern part of the Shenandoah Valley where Belle and her family called home, stood with the Union. In Martinsburg the Baltimore and Ohio Railroad, and the town's easy access to the Valley Pike, had made many of its over three thousand residents prosperous. It also made them loyal to the Union, which was made abundantly clear when Martinsburg was the only town in the Shenandoah Valley to vote *against* secession.

Belle and her family were not like most Martinsburg residents, though. They didn't put economics and profits ahead of their beliefs and stood firmly with the Confederacy.

Once Belle's composure was restored, her father squeezed her hands. "I trust you won't do anything foolish in my absence?" He lifted his eyebrows.

"When have I done something foolish?" she asked in an exaggerated southern accent.

Her father threw his head back and laughed. "That is a silly question for one with numerous foolish acts in her repertoire. I am sure you recall busting into a party in which you were not invited?" He cocked his head to await her response.

"I was a child then," Belle shot back. Feeling her face heat, she squared her shoulders and lifted her chin. "I am mature now."

He chuckled deep in his throat. "Yes, you were a child then. One of the most strong-willed children I have ever known. You did whatever it took to get your way." He leaned forward and chucked her under the chin.

"Riding your horse into a dinner party you were not allowed to attend because you were too young was bad enough. But shouting, 'My horse is old enough, isn't he?' to my guests, showed just how determined and hard-headed you were. And still are." He lowered his head, gazed into her eyes, then added, "Your mother and I were horrified, but your antics won the guests over. If I recall, you escaped punishment at their urging."

She huffed in a most unladylike manner. "You sent me away to school instead. To learn how to become a lady. I have done that, Father. As a debutante in Washington, I learned *so* much about our society and the politics that go with it." She cocked her head and waited for *his* response.

"That is true. I sometimes wonder if your education hasn't made you more determined than you were before. Knowledge is a powerful tool." He dipped his chin.

Indeed, it was. As a child she'd thrown many a tantrum to get her way. While in Washington, however, she'd learned to use her femininity. With the boys and young men, a few batted eyelashes and a coy smile got her whatever she wanted. Even with her overlarge, hooked nose and ordinary brown hair, she managed easily. With her father, it was tears that turned him to putty in her hands.

Her father put on what Belle called his "stern" face. "Do as I tell you and stay out of trouble. I shan't be here to save you from yourself." He lifted his brows.

"Haven't I proven that I've matured since my return? I nurse those in need. I have raised funds for our cause. And sewn clothing for the men going to fight for that cause. What more must I do to demonstrate that I am a grown woman and should no longer be treated as a child?"

He touched her cheek and grinned. "My darling Belle. I am proud of what you have done, but some things never change. That is you. Whether you are twelve, twenty or even forty, you will want what you want and do whatever you must to get it. You've proven it so too many times. And you are a master at it," he added with a wink. "You will behave?" he asked one last time.

She opened her mouth, took a deep breath, then blew it out. She closed her eyes and nodded. "Yes, Father." She slid her hand behind her back and crossed her fingers. "I promise."

Two Weeks Later (May 23rd)

Belle gripped the rail of the second-floor balcony. Her neighbors were marching up and down the streets of Martinsburg, protesting the Confederate presence at nearby Harper's Ferry. They may as well have been protesting her father, among Colonel Jackson's recruits there. Most of Martinsburg's citizens were well aware of Benjamin Boyd's allegiances. They'd certainly made their disgust known to Belle and her mother whenever they were in town with their unveiled criticism, turned backs and hateful scowls.

Along with today's protests, the citizenry of Martinsburg was also voting in a special statewide referendum to repeal secession in all of Virginia. The residents of her home town were making it perfectly clear they intended to vote for repeal, despite the fact that the rest of Virginia had voted for secession once, and would do so again.

As the day progressed, Colonel Jackson's soldiers began to fill the streets. Was her father among them?

Mid-morning, the front door opened. Benjamin Boyd stomped into the house his arms thrown wide. "I'm home!"

Belle dropped the book she'd been reading in the front room and flew into his arms. "You're here. We hoped you would be with the soldiers when they marched into town. Oh, Father, I'm so glad to see you. We've missed you." She hugged him again.

Belle's mother, her little four-year-old brother, Billy, and their house girl, Eliza, hurried into the room. When Billy spotted his father, he ran to him and flung himself into his arms.

Benjamin Boyd lifted Billy above his head and twirled him in a circle. The boy giggled uncontrollably until Benjamin pulled his son to his chest. He hugged the boy until he squeaked, then kissed his baby cheeks and set him on his feet, ruffling his hair as the child gained his balance.

Mary stepped to her husband. "Hello, Benjamin." Her voice cracked, as though she was trying not to cry.

Benjamin swept her into his arms, hugged and kissed her until she staggered back with a silly look on her face. "It is good to see you, Mary." His voice was deep with emotion.

Billy stood beside his father, looking up between his parents he asked, "Can I go play now?"

"Of course, you may." Mary bent over and kissed the top of his head. "Have fun."

The boy hurried to Eliza, took her hand, and the two disappeared from the room.

Benjamin pulled Belle close again and kissed her on the forehead. He shut the door with his foot then stepped between mother and daughter, his arms around their shoulders as he guided them into the room.

"Are the troops here to stop the referendum?" Mary asked when the three were seated, Belle's mother and father on the settee in front of the window and Belle in a winged-back chair across from them.

Belle stared at her father, so handsome in the butternut uniform her mother had made for him.

He shook his head. "No, we didn't come to *stop* the vote. We're here to quell any violence before it erupts. Hence our show of force. We shall guard the voting locations to ensure peace throughout the day."

"I don't care why you're here, I'm glad you are," Belle told him.

"I'm here right now to tell you what is happening so you will stay inside and away from trouble." He looked pointedly at Belle.

Belle harumphed. "I haven't been in any trouble since you left, Father, like I promised." She crossed her arms over her chest, as though his insinuation hurt. She'd become quite adept at making men feel guilty for any little infraction.

"I'm glad to hear that. I knew I could count on you to do as you promised."

Belle felt a twinge of guilt.

"How long can you stay?" Mary asked.

"I have the day. I must report back tonight."

"If a day is all we have, we'll take it," his wife said.

"Yes, we will," Belle parroted.

The residents of Martinsburg voted three-to-one that day against secession. Belle came to the full realization that she lived in a town of traitors. But no matter how much the citizens of Martinsburg protested or which way they voted, the rest of the Valley and Virginia had spoken.

Secession stood.

A Month Later (June 20th)

Belle watched from the front room as more troops from the Virginia Infantry marched into Martinsburg.

"What are they doing here?" she asked her father when he stepped beside her in the sitting room. He'd been allowed to visit often while the 2nd Virginia had remained in town.

He heaved a sigh. "Looks to me like the folks of Martinsburg are about to pay for their indiscretions."

"What does that mean?" Belle asked with uncertainty.

"Since the citizens chose to stand with the Union in an attempt to repeal secession, Colonel Jackson is going to show them Confederate strength."

"What does he intend to do?"

"It would be my guess that he plans to destroy the round house—"

"The what?" Belle interrupted.

"The round building at the depot. It's where they house the trains. If they dismantle the tracks, destroy the railroad buildings, locomotives, and hundreds of cars kept there, Martinsburg will be of no further use to the Union."

"Oh, my," was all she said. Belle didn't agree with how the town had voted in the referendum. But she did have friends here. She frowned. Well, she used to. Although she was now a pariah because of her beliefs, she didn't want to see the town destroyed and the citizens thrown into poverty. But they'd voted against the rest of the state. Put their ideals above everyone else's.

The more she thought about it, the less she cared. She had no reason to defend any of their actions or worry what those actions would cost them. They'd deserted her and her mother.

Her chin lifted a notch when she recalled an incident in the town square that had sent her mother home in tears. Women she'd been friends with for years had turned their backs on her. They'd refused to acknowledge her presence when she spoke to them. It had hurt Belle more to see her mother so distraught than if she, herself, had been snubbed.

Belle shrugged. "Well, they made their bed, now they must lie in it."

Her father grinned. "Spoken like a true Rebel." He gave her shoulders a squeeze. "I must go, but I'll be back. The troops will be here awhile. It'll take some time for them to destroy all Martinsburg has to offer."

Two Weeks Later (July 4th)

Belle and her mother stood on the second-floor balcony looking out over Martinsburg. "Those damn Yankees are like a horde of ants scurrying through the streets," Belle murmured with undisguised disdain.

"Maria Isabella Boyd. You watch your tongue," Belle's mother chastised. "You were raised better than to speak in such a vulgar manner."

"I apologize, Mother." Belle forced herself to sound contrite, although she didn't feel the least bit sorry for her words or her tone. "You must admit that since claiming victory at Hoke's Run two days ago, the Federals have taken whatever they want from their *Federal* supporters here in town. If these were Confederates, I could see their lack of restraint in their plunder. But this town supports their cause, and they well know it." Her heart stilled, recalling her father would have been with Jackson's command at the recent battle. Had he survived? The initial numbers said few men were killed. She gave up a silent prayer he was not one of them.

Her anger rose again when she looked down at the streets below. "They take whatever they want." She shook her head in disgust. "And look at how the Union-minded residents of Martinsburg still fawn over them. It shames me."

"Belle, you must keep those opinions to yourself," her mother hissed. She looked around to see if anyone below was close enough to hear her daughter's loudly voiced criticisms.

"I will not. Just because the majority of folks in Martinsburg side with the Union, does not mean I must. And I won't." She snapped her mouth shut. Her eyes grew wide and her chin jerked up and down. "I know exactly how to let them know where I stand in this...this War of Rebellion," she spat out. "What we good Confederates prefer to call the War of *Northern Aggression*."

"Do not do anything foolish, Belle. You promised your father." Her mother gave her a stern look.

"I have every right to do what I intend," Belle snapped.

"And will *your* actions cause *us* regret?" her mother asked with a glare.

Belle didn't answer. Instead, she grabbed up her skirts and charged into the house.

A half hour later, the Stars and Bars hung in both windows of her bedroom.

"This," her mother waved her hand at the flags when she entered the room, "is foolish. The town is swarming with Federals and you dare to fly two Confederate flags for all to see?"

Anger was heavy in her mother's tone, but Belle chose to ignore it. "I am an American citizen. Well, I was until we seceded," she added with a shrug. "But if those Yankees believe so strongly in the laws of the United States, then I have every right to display those flags."

Mary Boyd sighed heavily. "This statement you have made is not good, Belle. Not good at all. I fear it will bring trouble to our door."

Belle again chose to ignore her mother. She hurried down the hall to the sitting room. There she could watch the silly residents of Martinsburg fuss over their Union invaders.

Belle and her mother were in the sitting room a few hours later working on their stitchery when a pounding on the front door drew their attention.

"Who could that be?" Uncertainty was heavy in Mary's voice.

"I don't know, but I shall find out." Belle put her sewing aside, got to her feet, and grabbed the pistol hidden in the side table. She slipped the gun in her pocket and went to answer the door. She thrust it open to find a federal soldier standing on the porch. He swayed slightly, giving Belle the impression he was, perhaps, drunk.

Her eyes were drawn to what he held in his hands. "What, pray tell, do you intend to do with that?" Belle thrust her chin toward the American flag.

"I intend to hang it." He pointed at the balcony above his head. "Up there."

"You cannot," Belle challenged.

"I can and I will." He pushed his way into the house.

"How dare you!" she shouted when he whirled on unsteady legs to face her. "You have no right."

Her mother stepped beside Belle and linked her arm in hers. "What is the meaning of this intrusion? You have not been invited into our home. Leave this instant."

The soldier swayed and grinned maliciously. "I'm not going anywhere. Not till I do what I came to do."

"And what is that?" Mary squared her shoulders.

Belle flung her hand at the flag. "He intends to hang that on our balcony."

Mary stared a moment then lifted her chin. "I say again. You were not invited into our home. And you have no right to hang that anywhere on our property." She thrust her hand toward the flag. "Remove yourself this instant!"

The soldier stepped menacingly toward the two women. "Being that this town is under Federal control, I intend to remove the rags you call flags hanging in the windows of this house."

Belle unlinked her arm from her mother's and took a step closer. "We have the right to fly whatever flag we want in our home. Isn't that what your precious Constitution tells us?"

"You don't have that right anymore. Not since Virginia seceded." He'd spit out the words like there was something rotten in his mouth. He lifted his flag. "Your family seems to be the only one in town that has a problem flying *this* flag." He thrust it toward her. "I intend to correct that by removing the others and putting this one up instead."

"We will not fly that...that thing," Belle ground out.

"I shall not make the request again. Remove yourself, and it, from our property." Mary waved her hand at him and his flag.

He stepped to within a foot of Belle's mother, then leaned closer, putting his face in hers. "I don't take orders from a southern whore."

Belle blinked furiously at the affront.

The soldier straightened his shoulders then drew his hand back as though to strike her mother.

Belle didn't hesitate. She pulled the pistol from her pocket and shot him in the chest.

His eyes widened. His mouth opened and a hiss escaped. He looked down and touched the spot where blood spread across his shirt. Surprise filled his eyes when he looked up. His lips moved, but nothing came out. He shook his head then dropped to the floor like a stone.

Mary stared down at the fallen soldier. "Dear Lord, Belle. What have you done?"

"He insulted you in the most vulgar manner. I could not ignore his slur upon your person. When he raised his hand to strike you—"

Before Belle finished her statement, dozens of Federal soldiers charged into the house. The injured man was carried away under the care of a doctor. When he died several hours later, Belle and Mary Boyd were placed under house arrest.

"You've done it now, Belle," her mother cried when a guard positioned himself outside the front door.

Belle glared at her mother. "I was defending your honor. That man insulted you in the worst way. He intended to hit you. I could not allow that." She stared a moment then added, "I would do the same thing again if another fool came to our door and spoke to you or threatened you in such a vile manner.

"We have a right to defend ourselves," Belle continued. "He was drunk and unsteady on his feet. When he lifted his hand to strike you…I feared what he might do. To both of us." She paused a moment then added. "All we need do is tell the truth. We feared for our safety."

Mary blinked and nodded. "I did feel threatened." She took a calming breath then said, "The truth shall prevail."

"Yes, it shall," Belle mumbled, although not convinced the truth was all they would need. They were under Union control and she'd killed a Union soldier. Would they even listen to the truth?

The following morning, they were taken under guard to the courthouse to face a board of inquiry. When mother and daughter related the events to the board and the dead soldier's commanding officer, it was ruled the shooting was in self-defense and justified. They were sent home. However, upon their arrival, sentries took position around the house.

Although they'd been vindicated, their home was now a prison.

Ten Days Later (July 14th)

With as much sweetness as Belle could summon, she asked the guard standing inside the back door, "Would you like more tea?" She batted her lashes and smiled. She'd been flirting shamelessly with all the guards since her arrest almost two weeks ago, but this one had been the most receptive to her charms. All it took was a little food, some tea, and a few winks and smiles. In their previous conversations, Belle had gleaned information about Federal troop movements and strengths. She intended to get that information to those it would benefit. The Confederacy.

"Thank you, Miss, but no. If I drink much more, well…" His face pinkened.

"You may call me Belle. It is my given name." She smiled again and tilted her head in a shy manner. Men thought women were silly. It was men who were silly. She'd learned in Washington that, even if a woman wasn't beautiful, it didn't take much to turn their heads, as she proved over and over.

"I should get back to my post." He handed her the cup and saucer.

"Your post." Belle tittered with laughter. "It sounds so…formal. Your post is my back door."

He frowned. "I know, Miss Belle, and I'm sorry for it. But orders are orders." He spun on his heel to go outside, then paused and turned back. "I fear this is the last I shall see of you."

Belle put her hand to her chest, as though surprised. In reality, she hoped he might reveal something of importance to her. "Pray, why is that?"

"We're pulling out in the morning."

Belle forced her eyes to fill with tears. She lifted her hand toward his face to caress his cheek, then jerked it away, as though to check herself from such an improper action. She glanced away then said, "I shall be sorry to see you go." She bit her lower lip. "Where are you going?" she asked after another pause.

The young soldier drew up his back and shook his head. "I can't tell you that."

She withdrew a step and pretended his statement had hurt her feelings. "What could I possibly do with such information? I am under guard day and night. I am merely..." She made her lips quiver, "Afraid for what might happen. To you," she added with an expression of concern.

His face softened. "I don't guess it could do any harm." He stepped back inside then strode to the other side of the room. He poked his head out the inner door, checked the hallway, then went outside and looked around. When he stepped back into the kitchen, he said, "Word is our destination is Harper's Ferry, but we're headed south first."

Belle's heart thudded, but she kept the forced smile on her face. She listened long enough for him to tell her exactly when they were leaving and where they were going.

The information she'd gleaned from the silly guards was enough to make her want to test a theory she'd been mulling in her head for days. If a good, southern girl was found alone on the road, would she be stopped, searched or detained? After all, it was unheard of for a soldier, or any man for that fact, to lay hands on a lady.

Once Belle had said her tearful farewell to the guard, she hurried up the stairs. Although she knew death was a possible penalty if caught in the act of espionage, she was compelled to try. Her information could save dozens of lives. Perhaps even her father's.

Harper's Ferry, twenty miles south and west, and controlled by the Confederacy only weeks ago, was now held by Yankees. As far as Belle knew, Colonel Jackson and his men had probably moved south to Winchester. She had to find out for sure in order to relay her information.

Belle went into her room and looked for something in which to conceal her rather large message. She spotted a box that held a watch. She opened it, pulled out the watch and the inside packing. "This will do just fine. I'll put the note in the bottom, put the packing and watch back in, and no one will ever know," she whispered to the empty room.

The following morning after the soldiers vacated the premises, she saddled her mare and set out to bring her information to Commander Jackson—hopefully in Winchester.

She'd gone only a few miles when a Federal picket stopped her.

"What are you doing out on the road alone, Miss?" the soldier asked.

"I...I had a fight with my parents." Belle made her voice crack. She dabbed at her eyes. "I needed to get away to clear my head."

"You do realize there's a war going on and that there are troops, from both sides, spread across this valley?"

Belle sniffled and pulled a handkerchief from her reticule. She patted her nose and forced more tears. "I only wanted to escape the house. My father can be so unyielding..."

The soldier reached up. "Please hand me your bag."

"My bag?" Fear zipped up her spine. The watch box was too large to conceal on her person and she hadn't had time to stitch it into her petticoats. So, she'd hidden the message in the bottom of the box and put it inside her reticule, confident she would not be stopped or searched. She was, after all, only a mere girl. "Why on earth do you want to see my bag?" She tried to sound outraged, innocent, and not very bright at the same time.

"Hand it down, please." The gray-headed soldier wiggled his fingers.

With a hard swallow, she put the bag in his palm—and prayed.

He pulled out the watch box and set it aside to search the rest of the contents.

Belle's heart slowed. He wasn't interested in the watch case.

After placing everything back inside, he reached for the box, studied it a moment, then opened it.

Belle's heart started slamming in her chest again. Would he remove the packing and find the missive hidden in the bottom? She smiled sweetly to offset the frightened twitch of her lips. Tried to engage him in conversation to divert his attention, but he was intent on checking the package.

He cocked his head, removed the watch and packing. His eyes snapped up when he saw the folded parchment paper on the bottom. "What's this?" His tone was hard.

"Why...I don't know what you're speaking of?" Belle said in an offended tone.

He pulled out the paper and waved it in front of her. "This is what I'm talking about." He unfolded it and studied the contents of the information she'd gleaned from her unsuspecting guards.

Belle wanted to bolt, but he was holding the horse's bridle with his other hand.

"You're going to have to come with me, Miss."

Hope fled. She'd been caught. Her only thought now was how to get out of it.

Belle was returned home later that same day under guard. When Mary Boyd met Belle and the four soldiers in the front room, Belle flung herself, sobbing, into her mother's open arms. Her tears were as much for show for her captors, as to release the uncertainty of her churning stomach.

"We caught your daughter on the road with this." The captain thrust the box holding the message Belle had been caught carrying at her mother.

Mary set her daughter back. She looked up and said, "It's a box. What is this about?" Her eyes were wide with doubt.

"They're...they're accusing me of spying, Mother," Belle cried out as though the accusation wounded her deeply. "Have you ever heard anything so silly?" she wailed.

"That cannot be true," Mary responded.

"The evidence is right here." The captain pulled the paper out of the box and waved it in front of Mary's face.

SNIPPETS-Book Two   *D.L. Rogers*

"I...I received the watch as a gift," Belle lied. As though it made a difference where the box came from. "I don't recall from whom," she added, using the defense she had formulated during the trip home. "Perhaps the message was in there when I received it. I do not know anything about it," she finished with an unladylike sniffle.

"There, Sir. My daughter is innocent. She knows nothing about a message and she is certainly *not* a spy. That is the most foolish thing I've ever heard. She's a child."

"She is no child," the soldier responded in a hard tone. "And the information on this parchment was only released within the last few days. If she received the watch as a gift, how could that be?" he asked.

Belle stomped forward in indignation. "I don't know how that paper got in there." She forced sobs from deep in her belly.

The officer shook his head and frowned. "Who was this friend?"

Belle pushed out more tears. "I told you I don't recall."

"You don't recall?" he aped. "I think you're ly—"

Mary stepped in front of him. "Do not speak the words you intend to say, Sir! If my daughter says she does not recall, she does not recall." Mary Benjamin stared the man down.

Belle was more than thankful she hadn't told her mother about her plan. When she pled her daughter's innocence, she fully believed it.

The captain drew in a heavy breath. He studied Belle. "Very well," he finally said. "Although I don't believe a word you say, I shall not take this further." He stepped toward Mary. "I suggest you impress upon your daughter the dangers of playing with fire. If she continues to do so, she may get burned." He turned on his heel, waved his hand for the others to follow, and exited the house.

The next day, Belle was on her way to live with her aunt and uncle in their hotel in Front Royal, a tiny town with less than five hundred residents forty miles south.

November 1861

Belle had been with her Aunt Rebecca and Uncle John in Front Royal for three months. She was bored beyond comprehension. Her cousins, John, the same age as Belle at seventeen, Anna, fifteen, and Virginia, twelve, tried to keep her entertained, but nothing in this little town held her interest.

A knock on her bedroom door drew Belle's attention. "Come in."

Her Aunt Rebecca entered with an envelope in her hand. "A letter has arrived from your father."

Belle jumped from the chair where she'd been staring out the window. She snatched the letter and tore it open.

My Dearest Belle,

I hope this finds you well. I miss you, your mother and brother terribly, and hope to see you soon.

I have learned General Jackson, "Stonewall" as he's been called since his magnificent stand at Manassas in July, has been promoted, yet again, to Major General. His command, to which I am attached, is relocating to nearby Winchester. We shall be there by the time you receive this letter.

Since I shall be close, I should like to see you. Please make arrangements with my brother to accompany you there. I anxiously await your arrival.

Father

Belle jumped up and down like a little girl, the letter crushed in her hand near her heart. "Father wants me to visit him in Winchester."

"Do you think that's wise?" Rebecca asked.

"Father wants me to go," she responded defensively. "Besides, the Yankees have been scarce since they left Harper's Ferry at the end of August. We can be in Winchester by noon if we leave early and ride hard."

"And who do you intend to escort you?" Rebecca's tone was wary.

"Father told me to ask Uncle John." Without giving her aunt a chance to argue, Belle hurried from the room. "I'm going to find him right now and ask him to accompany me," she called over her shoulder as she disappeared down the hall.

Barely before dawn the next morning, Belle and her uncle set out on horseback for Winchester. They arrived by mid-afternoon. When stopped by two sentries outside of town, her uncle showed him the letter. They passed without hindrance. Of course, Belle's flirtatious manner with both guards aided in their cause.

Belle and her Uncle John were led to her father's tent. She rushed into his arms when he pushed through the flap.

"I see you received my message," Benjamin said after the two parted. He turned to his brother, shook hands and said, "Thank you for bringing her."

"We wouldn't have come if I didn't feel it was safe."

Benjamin nodded and hugged Belle again.

They spent the afternoon talking about family and the war, until the conversation turned to Belle's attempt at spying.

"What you did was very risky," her father said, but without reproach she noted with surprise.

"I know, but the Confederacy needed the information." She paused and bit her lower lip. "I had to try. I only wish I had succeeded."

Her father took a deep breath. He held it a moment then asked, "Would you like to try again?"

John jerked upright and squared his shoulders. "Benjamin, you can't be serious. Do you realize what you're asking her to do?"

Belle held her breath, uncertain what to say or do. She stared at her father a moment then said, "I don't understand. You've always been so protective of me. Warned me not to find trouble. Now you want me to walk into it?"

Belle's father closed his eyes and nodded. "I do. I've watched you work your special magic since you were a child. Now that you're older, you can use that. Men think you're an empty-headed female who couldn't possibly understand the war, let alone carry important information. But we know better," he finished with a wink and a smile.

Belle's father and uncle debated the issue for several minutes before she stood and said, "I can do it. I'll do whatever I can to bring victory to the Confederacy."

Both men stopped talking and stared at her.

"I can do it," she said again. "I know I can. And I won't get caught this time."

"You were sure you wouldn't get caught the last time," John reminded her.

"I'll take the time to sew the missives into my corset or undergarments before I attempt to deliver them. If stopped, I'm merely a young girl out for a ride. My virtue wouldn't be questioned and no soldier would dare search my person."

"I disagree." John's tone was hard.

"I don't," her father said in the same, harsh tone. "She could travel the roads without being stopped because she is a girl. And if she is stopped, she is very good at talking her way out of any situation. She's done it too many times to count through the years."

Belle flushed with her father's praise. She didn't understand his change in thinking, but was happy to do as he asked. For the Cause. "I'm willing, Father. Tell me what you want me to do."

With a huff, John let his shoulders sag. He shook his head.

"I want you to act as a courier between General Jackson and General Beauregard," her father said.

"I think you're making a mistake, but she's your daughter," John snapped before Belle could respond.

Belle walked to her uncle. "I can do this, Uncle John. I must do this. It's my way of contributing to the Cause."

"Must I remind you, both of you, that you're risking your life. If you're caught..." John pursed his lips and shook his head again.

"I know what can happen and I'm willing to take the risk. Our troops need good information. If I can get it to them, then I shall. It could be the difference between winning a battle and losing it. Saving Confederate lives." She stood firm, despite her uncle's scowl.

"Benjamin, you can't let her do this," John protested again.

Benjamin Boyd shook his head. He looked at Belle and smiled. "I think it's too late. I believe my daughter has already made up her mind."

"I have, indeed. When do I start?"

Belle studied the message General Jackson put in her hand the following morning. It was just a piece of folded parchment paper. What did it say? Would delivering this make a difference? She hoped it, and she, would make a great deal of difference in the war effort.

"I thank you, Sir, for giving me the chance to aid the Cause."

"Young lady, you are very brave, but I must be sure you understand exactly what you're doing."

"I do, Sir, and I'm still willing."

"Very well then. I've procured a conveyance for your travels between here and General Beauregard's camp." He waved his hand at a small buggy nearby. A horse was hitched to it and stood ready to go.

Belle had never felt so honored. "Thank you, again, Sir." She curtsied.

He nodded formally.

She ducked into her father's tent and hid the message inside her corset, confident she wouldn't be searched.

Her father helped her up onto the buggy seat. He took her hand and squeezed it once she'd settled. "Remember, you are a lady if you come upon any Federals. Don't forget it for one moment. You're visiting your aunt and uncle in Front Royal from Martinsburg, where secession has been voted down twice. You wholeheartedly agree. Make anyone who stops you believe that their cause is yours.

"If you're stopped by Confederates," he continued, "tell them you're going to visit your father in camp. No matter who stops you, remind them you are a lady and, as such, you should be allowed to pass. Use tears like you do on me if you must," he added with a wink. "Use your youth. Be the empty-headed female you're expected to be. Whatever it takes, make them believe you are an innocent. And by God, don't give them a reason to suspect anything is amiss. Be cordial and friendly as a lady always is." He lifted his brows.

Belle grinned and touched her father's cheek. "I *have* done this before, Father. Men are..." she paused, unsure whether to say what she wanted to her father.

"Go on." His voice was deep with a trace of humor.

"Men are witless when it comes to women. I mean, look at me, Father, I'm not beautiful, but men fawn over me because I'm tall, well dressed, and know how to make them feel special." It was Belle who winked this time. "Trust me. I know what to do."

Her father shook his head. "I don't doubt it. If I did, I wouldn't allow you to do this. You are and always have been a master of manipulation. I wouldn't be surprised that you weren't manipulating me into allowing you to do this."

She laid her hand across her heart and blinked. "Father, you asked me, remember?" She tilted her head.

"As I said, a master manipulator. Now go. And be safe." He kissed her hand.

Her uncle rode up beside his brother. "I hope you don't regret this."

"She's a strong girl. And smart. She'll do well," Belle's father assured his brother.

"I pray you're right. I'm glad it's not me that's betting on my daughter's life that she doesn't get caught."

Before heading back to the family's hotel in Front Royal, Belle and her uncle made a detour to General Beauregard's camp, the directions given to them before their departure from Winchester. They'd been issued passes for the sentries to let them through. After giving General Beauregard the missive from General Jackson, Belle boarded the buggy and she and John started home.

A feeling of worth filled her chest. Today, she'd made a difference. How many Confederate soldiers' lives might she save with the information she'd passed on? She might never know, but intended to do the same tomorrow, the next day and the next.

All the way home, Belle pondered how best to gather information that would benefit Generals Jackson and Beauregard. When the idea struck, she put it into motion.

The next day she gathered up whatever food she could get her hands on, without leaving her uncle's household in need. She packed it into several baskets, loaded it into the buggy and started out.

"Halt! Who goes there?" a sentry called when she neared the Union camp.

Belle reined the horse to a stop and flashed her most winning smile. "Good day. My name is Belle. I've come with food for your soldiers. Something other than beans and hardtack." She paused then added, "I also bring companionship." Her lips curled again and she fluttered her eyelids.

The guard lowered his rifle and took a step back. "I must search your baskets, Miss. You understand?"

"Of course. Please. Take them." She handed the three baskets to the sentry. "I want to help in any way I can. If it's by giving a little food and some companionship to our courageous troops, then my task shall be fulfilled," she finished with a flourish.

The baskets were checked and handed back to her. "You're free to go." The guard glanced up, a sheepish look on his face. "Might I be allowed to partake a little something from the bounty you're carrying?"

"Certainly. Take whatever you like. There's plenty." She handed one of the baskets to him, another wide smile on her face.

From that day forward, Belle visited the Federal camps every day. She strolled amongst the men. Offered food and company whenever anyone would take it. And she gleaned information from bits and pieces of conversations she overheard or enjoyed. Information she passed on.

Belle had been carrying communications between the generals for several months now, when she came upon two Union soldiers on one of her runs.

As she slowed, one grabbed the horse's bridle. The buggy jerked to a halt.

Belle made her chest rise and fall. She shook her head as though distressed. "Oh, thank goodness I have found someone." Her voice was frightened, soft and feminine. "I can't seem to find my way home. I have been lost for hours."

"Where is home?" one soldier asked. His eyes were bright as he studied Belle's face and stylish clothing. Or was he eying the figure hidden beneath that clothing? Belle hoped so with an internal giggle.

"Front Royal," she replied sweetly. "The day was so beautiful I went for a ride. I've only been here a short time, visiting my aunt and uncle you see, and lost my way." She shook her head and brought her handkerchief to her nose. "I am so embarrassed."

"Don't be, Miss. It's easy to get lost on these roads. It would be our honor to escort you home," the second soldier said.

"Oh, would you?" Relief was heavy in her voice. "That would be so kind of you."

The two soldiers mounted their horses and turned up the road in the direction of Front Royal. Belle followed, as though unsure where she was. But she *did* know where she was. She pointed this way and that, as though slowly recalling which direction she needed to go to get home.

Before the soldiers realized it, they came face to face with the sentries of a Confederate camp.

"Well, well, well, look who's come to grace our camp with her wit and beauty," one of the Confederate guards said. "Come on over, boys. See who's here, and what she's brought for us," he called to several other soldiers standing nearby.

"Why Miss Belle. It is good to see you. And what have we here?" The second guard waved his carbine at the two Union soldiers who sat their mounts, their mouths agape, their eyes filled with fear. They tried to turn their horses to run, but the bridles were in the grips of two Confederate privates.

She waved her hand in dismissal at the Federals and nearly snorted. They had proven, yet again, that all it took was feminine charm to shatter a soldier's armor.

"We'll take care of them, Miss Belle. You go on your way now," the first sentry told her.

"Thank you, boys. I'll see y'all soon." She slapped the reins and sent her mare and wagon toward Front Royal. She never looked back at the two gallant soldiers she'd left behind in the hands of their enemy.

Early May 1862

Belle wanted to scream. To tell the man to get out. Although it was a hotel, it was her family's home. But she held her tongue and forced a smile instead.

214

"To what do we owe this...honor, Sir?" John Boyd asked the Union general standing in the hotel's lobby.

The general stood, legs braced, studying the room. Finger by finger he pulled off his gloves then said with a nod, "This will do."

"Do, Sir?" John asked.

The general turned to John as though it was the first time he'd seen or heard the owner of the hotel he stood in. "I am General James Shields." He scanned the entryway again. "This will suffice as headquarters for myself and my staff."

Belle thought she would drop to the floor, both with fear and anticipation. The possibilities were endless as to what could happen with Union soldiers right here in her aunt and uncle's home! Good *and* bad.

"Of course, general, Sir, whatever we can do," John said cordially.

Rebecca stepped closer to her husband. "Whatever you need, we shall be happy to furnish in any way we can."

Belle curtsied. "We welcome your presence, Sir. I am pleased that you and your men are here." She fluttered her eyelids and let the slightest grin curl her lips before she looked away, her insides twisting like a butter churn. *Smile. Be gracious. Welcome them. Then use them.*

Welcome them Belle did. Day after day she feigned unwavering support for the Union. She brought the officers food in the main dining room. Engaged in mundane conversation to win their trust. She strolled the grounds with any officer who would share her company, which were many. Within days, she'd won them over, enough so that she was able to move about the hotel

215

without being stopped or questioned as to where she was going or why.

Her efforts were rewarded in mid-May when more officers arrived and gathered in the dining room. Belle brought them food before she was asked to leave and close the door behind her.

She hurried upstairs to the room directly above the dining area. She hid inside the closet and worked a small knothole in the floor into a larger one in order to hear the discussion below. Two hours later, the muscles in her legs and feet cramping, the men excused themselves.

It was time to take what she had learned to General Jackson via Colonel Turner Ashby, an oft-used liaison between her and General Jackson. She grabbed the fake pass she'd used many times that had given her entry into the Federal camps she'd visited in the last weeks— just in case. It would take too long using the buggy, so she saddled her mare and set out after darkness fell to reach Ashby's camp, the location familiar to her.

She rode the fifteen miles unmolested. The going was slow in the darkness and she arrived after midnight.

"I must see Colonel Ashby," she told the sentry who knew her by sight. "I have important information."

He let her pass and she rode straight to Ashby's command tent. She was stopped by another guard when she dismounted.

"I have important news for the colonel." She was winded with excitement. "I must get it to him immediately."

"Stay here." The sentry pushed through the flap and returned a few minutes later with a sleepy-eyed colonel.

"What do you have, Belle?" Ashby asked.

"General Shields and his officers had a war counsel at the hotel yesterday. They've received orders from General Banks to leave Front Royal. Soon. They intend to burn the bridges behind them, as well as destroy supply depots and transportation lines in their retreat. General Jackson must hurry to stop them."

"You've done a great service to your country, Belle," the colonel said. "You should start back right away to make it home before your absence is discovered."

Belle nodded. "Yes, Sir. Thank you, Sir." She hurried from the tent, mounted, and set off as fast as she could in the inky darkness, anxious to reach home before anyone knew she was gone.

May 23, 1862

Belle stared out the front window of the lobby of the hotel, waiting for General Jackson and his troops to arrive.

Her patience was rewarded. In the far distance she saw the line of gray clad soldiers heading toward town. She had to let them know the Federal positions and how many were in town. Her information could be critical to a victory for her countrymen.

Without forethought, Belle tied on her bonnet, grabbed up the skirts of her white day dress, and stepped onto the front porch. She sucked in a deep breath for courage then charged across the yard, into the street, and straight for the Confederate lines.

She ran like the devil was on her heels. It wasn't long before he was. Guns popped from the pickets as she raced past them. Her hat slipped from her head, the tie the only thing keeping it from flying away. She undid the bow as she ran, crushed the hat in her hand, and waved it at the approaching Confederates.

Rifle-balls slammed into the ground around her feet. Dust billowed into her eyes. She swiped it away and kept on, her only thought to reach General Jackson.

Bullets whizzed past her ears and face, but she would not be deterred. She stumbled when a bullet slammed through her wide skirts, but she didn't stop. She couldn't. The information she carried was too vital.

When Belle was near the front of the Confederate line, she waved her bonnet and shouted, "I have information for General Jackson!" She stopped long enough to refill her lungs then said to the officer who stepped forward to meet her, "Tell the general the Yankee force is very small. Tell him to charge right down and he will catch them all." She related further troop strengths, where the pickets were located and where the homes that housed the Federal headquarters were at.

The officer jumped on his horse and bolted to give his commander the information.

General Jackson's troops charged straight into the Federal defensive line that had formed on Richardson's Hill. But the Confederate army wasn't to be denied. After two hours of fighting, with more Confederate troops approaching from the west, the Federals gave up the fight and fled across the Shenandoah River. In their retreat, they attempted to burn the bridges behind them to cut off Rebel pursuit, but the flames were extinguished before much damage was done.

The Federals suffered nine hundred casualties that day and seven hundred men were captured.

Hours later, jubilant with the Confederate victory and her part in it, Belle greeted a soldier who entered the lobby of the hotel.

"I am looking for Miss Belle Boyd." He held a letter in his hand.

"I am Belle Boyd."

218

He jerked to attention and presented the letter with great flourish. "With General Jackson's compliments."

Heart pounding, Belle took the letter and thanked the messenger who turned on his heel and exited. She stood alone in the middle of the room and opened the envelope.

My Dearest Belle,

"I thank you, for myself and for the army, for the immense service that you have rendered your country today."

With Warmest Regards,

General Jackson

Belle sat down on the settee to keep her knees from buckling. The general went on to say that, for her contributions, he intended to award her the Southern Cross of Honor, the highest honor the Confederacy bestowed for valor.

Genuine tears filled her eyes, making it difficult to finish the letter. She swiped them away and read further. The general was also giving her honorary captain and aide-de-camp positions in his command.

Her eyes swam. Her head whirled. Her work had been rewarded beyond all expectations. All she'd ever wanted was to do her part for her country. To her delight, she'd succeeded.

*

August 29, 1862

Old Capitol Prison in Washington was the most dismal place Belle had ever seen.

The brick-walled structure at 1st and A Streets in Washington had once served as the temporary Capitol of the United States. Now it housed bugs, vermin, loneliness—and the increasingly infamous Belle Boyd.

Belle sat up on her threadbare cot and rubbed her throbbing temples. Her head always pounded when she considered how she'd come to be housed at one of the north's most notorious prisons.

Old Capitol had, at one time, housed Belle's hero, Rose Greenhow. However, Ms. Greenhow had been released in May of 1862, months before Belle's arrival.

Sometimes Belle wished Rose was still here. At least her loneliness might be assuaged by the companionship of another woman. But Belle hoped more that her hero was reprising her role as a Confederate spy, as she, herself, hoped to do again someday.

Belle closed her eyes and took a deep breath to ease the pain sweeping through her. She'd been arrested numerous times since the fight at Front Royal, but always managed to talk or flirt her way out of it. In the Yankees' frustration to capture her, a warrant for her arrest had been signed by the U.S. Secretary of War, Edwin Stanton.

Which led to the interest of none other than detective Allan Pinkerton. From what Belle had been told by the warden, after all it could do no harm telling Belle how she'd been arrested, Pinkerton had assigned three men to her case. Their goal was to find her and bring her to justice. Yankee justice.

How she'd wound up here stung her heart, and her pride, more than anything. Anger welled in Belle's chest. From the pain in her head or the pain in her heart, she didn't know. She just hurt.

She'd been here since July 29th when the man she'd given her heart to turned on her and had her arrested. One of the men Pinkerton had assigned to capture her.

Belle snarled and pushed her anger away. Today was going to be a good day. She'd been in this hellhole for a month, but she was being released in a prisoner exchange. She was both sad and happy. Sad because she'd allowed her heart to lead her head...and been betrayed. Which had landed her here. But today she was leaving, and that made her happy.

It was time to get back to work.

December 1863 (More Than a Year Later)

Belle dropped onto the cot with a groan. She laid her arm across her face and closed her eyes hoping sleep would come. Something skittered across her feet. She squealed, jumped up and danced around, slapping at her legs.

Day and night the vermin inside Old Capitol tortured Belle. At night, it was bedbugs. She awakened every morning covered with fresh bites. Of course, she could sleep on the cold, dirty floor instead, but that would be worse. It was the cot or nothing. At least with the bedbugs, she couldn't *see* what tormented her in her sleep. When she did sleep. It was the mice and bigger insects sharing her cell that made her want to curl into a ball in the corner.

After her release from Old Capitol in August of '62, she'd returned to Martinsburg to find it a Union stronghold. But that hadn't deterred her. She'd picked up where she'd left off, doing whatever she could to aid the Confederacy. She'd spied. Acted as a courier between camps. Whatever needed to be done, she did.

She grinned and pushed her matted, lice-filled hair off her face. "You're really famous now, Belle." Sarcasm was heavy in her voice as it bounced off the empty walls of her cell. She'd even talked herself into believing that, as long as she never gave her heart to another man, she would be safe.

She'd made a difference for the Confederacy for almost a year before being recaptured on one of her runs in July of '63. Sent back to Old Capitol, she'd been here nearly five months. Now all she fought were the bugs and rats that tortured her day and night instead of Yankees. Although, she did do her best to make the guards miserable as often as she could.

She sang Dixie in her cell. It gave her strength, but she also hoped to remind the other prisoners who they were and why they were here. Many joined her, the whole block singing at the top of their lungs until the guards threw water on them or cracked them with a stick or a whip. In the summer months, the water, stick or whip was worth the offence. Once it got cold, though, the water was awful, leaving the prisoner soaked and freezing. The singing would stop. Until Belle began again the next day, taking whatever punishment they gave her.

Belle picked up the cot and shook it to expel any critter that might have scurried inside. Confident there was nothing, she dropped it on the floor, straightened it, and sat down. She drew up her knees, wrapped her arms around them, and rested her chin on top. She considered her captors, especially the warden, who'd been vulnerable to her charms and allowed her special privileges others didn't get.

She'd been given fabric and needles to pass her time. After gathering enough cloth of various colors, she'd sewn together a Confederate flag, which she waved from her tiny window throughout the day. When the guards caught her and took it away, she pieced together another one.

Thoughts of her father crept into her mind and she sighed. Where was he? Had he been with General Jackson

at the Battle of Chancellorsville at the end of April? Had
he survived? Stonewall Jackson had not. A sob caught in
her throat. Scouting for the next day's battle after his
glorious victory earlier in the day, he'd been mistaken for
a Yankee spy and shot by his own men. Wounded in the
arm, the injury had festered, the arm removed. But the
general caught pneumonia and died eight days later. The
Confederacy mourned his death as they had never
mourned before.

The Yankees celebrated.

Belle had been on a run when she heard the news
of his death. The entire camp was grieving when she'd
arrived with her communiques. She'd dropped to the
ground, unable to stand as pain and anger tore through
her. She'd openly sobbed, her heart broken at the loss of
such a great man, and also fearing her father could be
amongst the dead.

She tried to get more comfortable on the cot, but it
was impossible. Her mind turned to her mother. Belle
wondered how she was adjusting to living in the new state
of *West* Virginia? On Belle's last trip to Martinsburg in
early July, shortly before her arrest, she'd learned the
unsettling news. After years of fighting over the ideals of
secessionism and slavery between eastern and western
Virginia, the issue had been resolved. On June 20, 1863,
West Virginia became a state. It unsettled Belle, knowing
her home was now in Yankee territory, but it also gave
her further incentive to continue her work.

Thoughts of Belle's family and home made her
melancholy. *I am strong,* she chastised. *I will not forget
who I am and what I've done for my country. I am the
Cleopatra of Secession. The Siren of the Shenandoah. The
Rebel Joan of Arc. They may have captured and
imprisoned me, but I will not be broken,* she promised the
empty room before drifting into an exhausted sleep.

She woke the next morning with a deep cough. Her insides churned. Chills wracked her body. Her head pounded as though a mallet swung back and forth in her brain. So weak, she barely made it to the bucket with diarrhea. After expelling everything inside her, Belle crawled back to the hated cot. Before she collapsed, she noticed several rose-colored spots on her forearm.

"Lord, no," she whispered. She knew now what ailed her. It had caused the deaths of many a man on both sides of the war.

Typhoid fever.

"No, no, no," she cried out in a strangled voice. No one heard. *I cannot die of this malady. I will not.* She fought against the darkness closing in.

Darkness won.

Belle's eyes fluttered open. The warden's face came into fuzzy view above her.

"Welcome back."

"How long...?" she managed her mouth so dry it felt like cotton bolls were stuffed inside.

"You've been feverish for several days," he told her.

"Typhoid?"

He nodded.

Belle forced her lip to turn up in a smirk. "In such a clean place? How could I have contracted Typhoid?"

"I see you still have your wit." He winked.

"If I lose that, I am nothing," she ground out. With great effort, she lifted her arms. The red spots were barely visible. Her headache and stomach pain were mostly gone. She coughed but that, too, was minimal. Only the muscle tenderness remained.

The warden touched her face, pushed an errant lock of dirty hair from her cheek. "We've been administering powdered opium. It seems to be doing the trick...when we can get you to drink. You're as hard-headed in your delirium as you are awake."

Belle smiled, coherent enough to realize he was giving her a back-handed compliment. She also knew what to do to capitalize on it. She let her eyes fill with tears. Made her lips tremble. She laid her hand over the warden's, still resting on her face. "I shall die here if I'm not released," she said barely above a whisper.

"You need not ply your wiles on me, my dear. Arrangements have already been made for your release." The warden's voice held a trace of humor. "I cannot stand by and let you die." His eyes sparkled with affection.

Belle cried openly as the warden promised her a quick discharge.

He shooshed her with a finger across her lips. His face solemn he said, "Although you're to be freed tomorrow, you won't be going home."

"Where am I to go then?" Uncertainty swept up her spine.

"You're being released because of your illness, but you're to be sent south. To Richmond."

Belle absorbed what she'd been told. Going to Richmond wouldn't be so bad, although she'd much rather go home where she could continue her work. In Richmond there would be nothing for her to do. After all, it was the Confederate capital. What spying *for* the cause could she do there?

May 8, 1864

Belle glided like a queen onto the deck of the *Greyhound.* Her passage to England aboard the Confederate blockade runner had been arranged by President Jefferson Davis himself.

"Welcome aboard, Miss Boyd," the seaman who greeted her said. "We're honored to have you with us. Your reputation precedes you," he added with a sweeping bow.

"Why, thank you, Sir. I am very happy to be here." She fluttered her lashes and smiled brightly when he stood erect again.

He offered his elbow. "May I escort you to your cabin?"

"I would be grateful, Sir," she answered with a coy tilt of her head.

A few minutes later she was settled in a moderate cabin where she would spend the next weeks crossing the Atlantic to London.

Dinner that night with the captain and officers was a festive affair. Belle was awed by the fine fare of pork, gravy, and all the side dishes one would find in an elegant restaurant. One of the officers even played the banjo and regaled her with his up-tempo tunes and soft ballads.

"This is a blockade running vessel, Miss Boyd," Captain "Henry" as the officers and crew called him, informed her when she inquired about the ship. "She's sleek and fast. Our mission on the outbound sail for England, is to protect her cargo of cotton, tobacco and turpentine from Union blockaders. Of course, detection must also be avoided on our return, whereupon her cargo is slated for the Confederacy. We are, however, able to gain a few ah...commodities for our own use. Thereby, we are afforded an enjoyable meal or two during our lengthy voyage." His eyes sparkled and Belle wasn't sure his procurement of *commodities* was done legally or illegally. However, that was not for her to judge, so she asked no further questions.

The officers treated her like royalty. She laughed more than she'd laughed in a very long time. She felt alive and useful. The dispatches she carried were of great importance to the Confederacy and she was honored President Davis had chosen her to deliver them.

She slept the second morning until a seaman arrived to escort her to breakfast. That afternoon, she strolled the deck on several occasions with different officers, all of whom fawned over her.

Dinner the second night was as elaborate as the first with roasted beef, potatoes, an array of vegetables and, of course, wine. Belle was asked about her adventures with the Confederacy, and she happily recounted them all.

The next day Belle was awakened by the sun blazing in through the small window of her cabin. She dressed, puzzled as to why no one had come to retrieve her for breakfast as they had the day before. It was nearly ten. *Have I been forgotten so soon? Breakfast must be long over by now.*

Belle left her cabin to seek out Captain Henry on the bridge. In the passageway, a biting wind swirled around her ankles. When she reached the upper floor, she jerked to a halt. Her eyes widened. Her breath caught. The chill streaking her back was not from the cold.

Yankees crowded the bridge of the *Greyhound*. Captain Henry and his officers stood huddled in front of them, pistols leveled at their chests. The crew sat on the floor of the lower deck, their hands and feet bound and under heavy guard.

Belle turned to run and bumped smack into a big Yankee. He grinned maliciously. "Ah, there you are Miss Boyd. We've been looking for you."

"You, you know me?" She swallowed hard, trying to dislodge the lump of fear that had formed in her throat.

227

"Oh, yes, I know you. We know well the notorious *Cleopatra of Secession*, one among many titles you've acquired during your reign of espionage."

Belle didn't know how to respond. Should she deny who she was? Cry? Flirt?

As though reading her mind, the man leaned closer. "Don't even try it." His mouth quirked in a sly smile. "Do not deny who you are. Do not cry and do not flirt. We know all your tricks." His voice was as soft as silk, as though to mock her.

"I…" She snapped her mouth shut when he waved his forefinger in front of her nose.

His eyes sparkled with mirth. He shook his head. "Ah, ah, ah."

She heaved a sigh of defeat. She'd been here before. She was caught like a fly in a web. Fighting against it would do no good.

Belle spent the rest of the morning in her cabin waiting. For what, she didn't know. She jumped to her feet when there was a knock on the door just after noon.

"Come in." She made her voice sound weak and frightened.

An officer entered, his hat in hand. He stepped toward her, clicked his heels and bowed. "Good afternoon, Miss Boyd. I am Lieutenant Samuel Hardinge."

Belle curtsied. "I am pleased to meet you, Sir." She studied the man who appeared to be the epitome of a gentleman with his immaculate attire, large, bright eyes and dark-brown hair that rested upon his shoulders. His refined manners were like that of a southern man, although he wore that damnable Union uniform. Her heart did a small tumble in her chest.

"I do not imagine there is much pleasure for you or your comrades in rebellion that this vessel is now under control of the *USS Connecticut* and the Union Navy."

"It is...a regret." Belle's voice was as sweet as punch. She waited a heartbeat then asked in a small voice, "What is to happen to me?"

"The ship will be taken up the coast to New York then Boston. The cargo will be removed and confiscated."

"And me?" she asked again. She lowered her lashes, lifted them, then gazed deeply into his face.

He cleared his throat. "I do not know."

He'd tried to sound hard, but Belle saw the crack in his exterior. His dark eyes were soft when he returned her gaze. It was time for her to draw on all the womanly ways she possessed.

"Shall I be forced to remain in this room for the entire journey north?" She paused a moment then added, "Must I take my meals here, as well? And what of sunshine and fresh air? I must have them else I shall wither away." She stepped closer and laid her palm on his chest. "Am I to perish for lack of these small comforts? And of loneliness?"

He didn't step back as she'd anticipated. Instead, he covered her hand with his. "You shall not want for anything, Miss Boyd. Be assured, I shall endeavor to keep you company throughout our trip."

Belle's heart thundered. She broke into false tears.

He immediately promised he would see to her comforts personally.

She smiled with victory when he turned away. It was so easy. She was already working her magic. And he didn't even know it.

*

During their more than week-long sail, Belle worked her spell on Sam Hardinge. Something else happened too. Her heart swelled with feelings for *him*. He was her enemy, and her savior.

It was obvious to Belle that Sam Hardinge was already in love with her. He confirmed it one night when they stood on the aft deck of the *Connecticut*, stars sparkling above them.

"I love you, Belle." He stepped closer and she allowed him to take her in his arms. "After you are released in Canada, go to London. Meet me there. And marry me."

Belle pulled back. Marry? Did he speak the truth? Could he really want her for a wife? Knowing what she was and the fact that they were on opposite sides of this war? Or was this a trick he was playing with her heart? She'd already been wounded once by that game.

"You don't believe I want you for my wife?" He took both of her hands in his. "I'll say it again. I love you, Belle. More than anything. Meet me in England after your release. We shall be married there. If you'll have me."

Belle studied the man who was laying bare his heart to her. He'd professed his love more than once. Could she believe him? She'd wound up in prison the last time she gave her heart to a man. This was a different man. An honorable man. One she chose to trust.

The *USS Connecticut* was at anchor in Boston. It was time for Belle to put her plan in motion. Tomorrow she would be exiled to Canada. Tonight, Belle had a role to play. A very important role. If she was caught, it could mean hers and Captain Henry's deaths.

"I find the air is much brisker than I imagined, Sam." Belle squeezed his arm. "Will you please get my wrap from my cabin?" They'd only just arrived on the upper deck for an evening stroll.

"Of course, my dear. I shall return shortly."

As soon as Sam left the deck, Belle plastered on her most feminine smile and started toward the guard posted near the gangplank. Throughout the journey, she'd been given open access to the ship. After all, where could she go except overboard, she'd pled to her captors early on. It wasn't unusual for her to stroll the deck at dusk with or without Sam Hardinge. Or be seen on the lower decks where Captain Henry was detained. She'd managed to sweet-talk her way inside his cabin earlier and, before leaving, had pushed a strip of wadded cloth from her petticoat into the door lock so it would close, but not engage. The plan was to wait until dark when he would slip out, hide on deck until she distracted the guard, then he would simply walk off the ship.

She waited until the opportune moment then pretended to trip over a coiled rope. With a loud wail, she flung herself to the floor a short distance from the guard.

The sailor hurried over to help her sit up, his back to the walkway. With embarrassment, she cried out, "Oh, my. How clumsy am I?" In her peripheral vision, she saw Captain Henry hurry along the rail to the un-guarded gangplank. He threw her a quick glance, saluted, and disappeared into the darkness.

Belle was lifted to her feet, crying out when she put weight on her foot. "I fear I have twisted my ankle."

"Let's get you to your cabin and off that foot, Miss Belle," the guard said.

She shook her head. "That's not necessary. Sam, I mean Lieutenant Hardinge, will return shortly. He can escort me to my cabin."

She smiled to keep from laughing out loud at the crestfallen look that fell over the guard's face. She hadn't lost her touch.

When Sam returned a few minutes later, she asked to walk along the railing on their way back to the lower deck. She assured Sam she would be fine as long as he guided her steps. Feigning disappointment, she told him, "I'd like to look out over the water. It is the last I shall see of it, since tomorrow I shall be on my way to Canada."

"And then to London," he reminded her.

"Of course. Then to London, where we shall meet and begin our lives together."

At the rail, she peered out into the night. In the distance, there was nothing but darkness.

Late August/September 1864

"Must you go back?" Belle smoothed an errant hair from Sam's forehead. "You've already been dismissed from the navy for allowing Captain Henry to escape. But you had nothing to do with it." She ran her hand over his face where they sat on the settee in the front room of their well-furnished house in London. "It was all my doing. I'm the one that helped him escape."

"I'm well aware, and so is the navy. How he walked off the ship without anyone stopping him doesn't matter. I was in charge."

"What do you hope to gain by going back now?"

"My pride, perhaps?"

"But you can't."

"I must try to clear my name. I had no idea you and Captain Henry had planned his escape. I was innocent, but because you were suspected, I took the full blame. Especially when I married you. It must look to one and all that I was complicit with the escape." He touched her cheek. "I would like to go back to at least plead my case and prove I'm no traitor."

Belle withdrew her hand and jumped to her feet. "And what do you think they'll do to you? Give you a medal for being honest, then trying to fix it by going back to plead your case? And being in love with a spy? Wouldn't that make you a traitor?" She knew her sarcasm hurt him, but she couldn't help it. She was happy. Really happy, for the first time in her life. She didn't want it to end because of her husband's misguided sense of honor. He should stay with her, forget what he'd done, and go on with the rest of his life. Their lives. But Sam was an honorable man. It was one of the reasons she'd fallen in love with him. As much as she wanted to, she couldn't deny him what he needed to do to assuage his own mind.

Sam stood and wrapped his arms around her shoulders. "Try to understand."

Belle's anger eased at his pleading. She touched his face. "I do understand. As I understood my father's reasons for marching off to war. And my need to spy for the Confederacy. My father is dead, and I can't go home. I don't want to lose you too. If you go back to face charges, I fear I shall never see you again." Genuine tears fell.

Sam pulled her into his arms and held her until she quit sobbing. His, "I leave in the morning," set her to crying all over again.

*

July-September 1865 in London, England

Belle looked around the room of her London home. Sam was gone, imprisoned in the United States for the past year.

233

She gazed down at the bundle in her arms, her daughter, Mary Grace Wentworth Fitzwilliam Belle Boyd Hardinge. Less than six months old, she had the dark brown hair and bright eyes of her father. She had inherited a rebellious streak a mile wide from her mother. It revealed itself often, even at this tender age. She cried to get her way and, when she didn't, she cried more and louder. As a woman without a husband at her side, Belle often indulged her to keep Mary's tantrums to a minimum.

Mary was silent now, only because her tummy was full and she was nice and warm. Belle stood and placed her daughter in the cradle, taking every care not to wake her. Belle breathed a sigh of relief when the child didn't wake up again.

She went back to the couch and picked up a book from the side table. Her book. The one she'd written while pregnant with Mary after Sam left. She'd written about her exploits as a spy during what most folks now called the American Civil War. She ran her hand over the title: *Belle Boyd in Camp and Prison.* She shivered. This was her story, published in May of 1865 for a London newspaper as a way to make ends meet in Sam's absence. It was a story she was proud of, despite those who challenged the truth of all she'd written.

She was The *Cleopatra of Secession.* The *Siren of the Shenandoah,* The *Rebel Joan of Arc,* and *La Belle Rebelle.* She was Belle Boyd...and she still had much to do.

Maria Isabella "Belle" Boyd
https://www.biography.com/military-figure/belle-boyd

Afterword

From the *American Battlefield Trust* (see references), Belle stated in her (sometimes fictionalized and occasionally challenged post-war memoirs) regarding the (drunken) soldier who "addressed my mother and myself in language as offensive as it is possible to conceive. I could stand it no longer...we ladies were obliged to go armed in order to protect ourselves as best we might from insult and outrage." According to the memoir, she did not suffer any reprisal for this action, "the commanding officer...inquired into all the circumstances with strict impartiality, and finally said I had 'done perfectly right.'"

Some accounts state it was the commanding officer who "judged" her and her mother as doing right, where other's state Belle and her mother were taken before an actual board of inquiry.

The town of Martinsburg, still Virginia at the beginning of the war, changed hands between the Union and Confederacy many times.

In some accountings of Belle's first attempt at spying during her "house" arrest, some say Eliza, a house slave, and others say a "friend/neighbor" was taking the information to Thomas Jackson when caught. Others merely state "After one such letter was intercepted, Boyd escaped punishment by feigning ignorance." (*Encyclopedia Virginia*, see references)

Some accountings of Belle's activities say she was in her aunt and uncle's hotel in Front Royal when she learned of General Shields's plans to vacate Front Royal by enlarging a knothole in the floor above the dining room where the Federal "war counsel" was being held. Others just say she was in a closet. Whether on the floor above or nearby, she enlarged a knothole to hear what was said. Some accounts say she found Colonel Turner Ashby, who was "scouting for the Confederates," and gave him the news. Some accounts say she went straight to General Jackson.

During the attack on Front Royal, from the *American Battlefield Trust*, Jackson's aide, Lieutenant Henry Kyd Douglas, described seeing "the figure of a woman in white glide swiftly out of town...she seemed...to heed neither weeds nor fences, but waved a bonnet as she came on." Boyd herself later wrote: "the Federal pickets...immediately fired upon me...my escape was most providential...rifle-balls flew thick and fast about me...so near my feet as to throw dust in my eyes...numerous bullets whistled by my ears, several actually pierced different parts of my clothing." Was this Belle's *embellished* story of what happened? Or the truth?

Also from the *American Battlefield Trust:* "Boyd's flirtations with Union officers, however, were her **strongest source of influence**. Contemporaries noted that 'without being beautiful, she is very attractive...quite tall...a superb figure...and dressed with much taste.'" On one occasion, she wooed a Northern soldier (one of her guards while under house arrest) to whom she (later?) wrote, "I am indebted for some very remarkable effusions, some withered flowers, and last, but not least, for a great deal of very important information...I must avow the flowers and the poetry were comparatively valueless in my eyes. I allowed but one thought to keep possession of my mind—the thought that I was doing all a woman could do for her country's cause."

On "Captain Henry's" escape from the *Greyhound*, it is historians' general consensus that Samuel Hardinge did aid in the escape, which states Belle distracted the guards while Captain Henry merely walked off the ship. However, Sam Hardinge's personal information states he was not complicit in the escape. Belle and Sam were, in fact, married on August 25, 1864 in St. James, Westminster, London, England, and he did return to the United States after their marriage. He was sent to prison and spent a year there before (reportedly) being released in 1865. Again, there are reports that he died shortly after his release in 1865/1866, but mystery surrounds his death. *Encyclopedia Virginia (see references)* states: "Her biographer Louis Sigaud believed that Hardinge died in 1865/66, but (according to other documentation) he was still living in 1870."

Per *WikiTree FREE Family Tree (see references)*: After her capture, while Belle was in Boston, a *Boston Post* reporter described her in this way: "She is a tall, well-formed, woman, blonde, [this reporter described her differently than most] and graceful in her manners. She converses freely and well and was evidently a female of intelligence and quick understanding."

Belle's father died on December 6, 1863, the same day he was mustered out of service with the Confederacy. It is assumed he died from injuries sustained while in service to the Confederacy.

Belle's life following Sam's incarceration in the United States and (supposed) death was by no means boring. From: *Belle Boyd—Britannica Online Encyclopedia*: Aside from writing *Belle Boyd in Camp and Prison (see references),* in 1866, Belle became an actress to support herself and her child, Mary Grace. She made her debut in *The Lady of Lyons* in Manchester, England. In 1868 she returned to the States and toured the south, appearing in *The Honeymoon*. Upon retiring from the stage in 1869, she married John Swainston Hammond, another former Union officer. They had four children before divorcing in 1884. Months later, she married an actor named Nathaniel High, seventeen years her junior. In 1886 she returned to the stage to re-enact her life during the Civil War. (Some say she was a lecturer on her Civil War exploits.) She died of a heart attack, in poverty, while performing in Wisconsin on June 11, 1900 at the age of 56. She is buried in Wisconsin Dells in the Spring Grove Cemetery there.

Resources

Maria "Belle" Boyd: American Battlefield Trust:
https://www.battlefields.org/learn/biographies/maria-belle-boyd

National Women's History Museum:
https://www.womenshistory.org/education-resources/biographies/isabelle-boyd

Wikipedia:
https://en.wikipedia.org/wiki/Belle_Boyd

Belle Boyd (1844-1900) - Encyclopedia Virginia:
https://encyclopediavirginia.org/entries/boyd-belle-1844-1900/

Britannica Online Encyclopedia:
https://www.britannica.com/print/article/76454

Biography.Com Website:
https://www.biography.com/military-figure/belle-boyd

History:
https://www.history.com/topics/american-civil-war/stonewall-jackson

History:
https://www.history.com/this-day-in-history/confederate-spy-belle-boyd-is-captured

Shenandoah Valley Battlefields National Historic District:
https://www.shenandoahatwar.org/stonewall-jackson

Intel.gov: https://www.intelligence.gov/evolution-of-espionage/civil-war/confederate-espionage/belle-boyd

Library of Virginia:
https://www.lva.virginia.gov/public/dvb/bio.php?b=Boyd_Belle

https://allthatsinteresting.com/belle-boyd-civil-war-spy

Isabella Maria (Boyd) High (abt. 1844-1900) / WikiTree FREE Family Tree:
https://www.wikitree.com/wiki/Boyd-4109

Made in the USA
Monee, IL
28 May 2023

34216483R00134